MARGUERITE HENRY'S

Ponies *of* Chincoteague

◆ Maddie's Dream ◆

CATHERINE HAPKA

Aladdin

New York   London   Toronto   Sydney   New Delhi

ALADDIN

An imprint of Simon & Schuster Children's Publishing Division
1230 Avenue of the Americas, New York, NY 10020
This Aladdin hardcover edition July 2014
Text copyright © 2014 by The Estate of Marguerite Henry
Jacket illustration copyright © 2014 by Robert Papp

Also available in an Aladdin paperback edition.
For information about special discounts for bulk purchases, please contact
Simon & Schuster Special Sales at 1-866-506-1949 or business@simonandschuster.com.
The Simon & Schuster Speakers Bureau can bring authors to your live event.
For more information or to book an event contact the Simon & Schuster Speakers Bureau
at 1-866-248-3049 or visit our website at www.simonspeakers.com.
Book design by Karina Granda
The text of this book was set in Adobe Caslon Pro.
Manufactured in the United States of America 1014 FFG
2 4 6 8 10 9 7 5 3
Library of Congress Control Number 2014936332
ISBN 978-1-4814-0337-5 (hc)
ISBN 978-1-4814-0336-8 (pbk)
ISBN 978-1-4814-0338-2 (eBook)

Maddie's Dream

◆ CHAPTER ◆
1

"OUT OF MY WAY!" MADDIE MARTINEZ burst through the back door into her family's sunny yellow-tiled kitchen. "I'm late!"

Maddie's older sister, Tillie, looked up from making a sandwich at the counter. "Whoa—it's summer vacation, remember? What's the rush?"

"My riding lesson's in less than an hour." Maddie didn't slow down as she headed for the stairs. "Where's Dad?"

"Doing laundry. I'll warn him that you're home."

"Thanks!" Maddie took the steps two at a time. The room she shared with Tillie was at the far end of the hall.

Maddie crossed her fingers, hoping Tillie hadn't gone on one of her cleaning sprees today. If she had, Maddie would never find her riding stuff.

Whew! The place looked the same as it had when she'd left for soccer practice. Tillie's half was spotless, her dresser and closet tidy and her bed neatly made with crisp white sheets and an assortment of throw pillows. Maddie's half looked as if a hurricane had just rolled through.

But Maddie knew where everything important was. Her breeches were draped over her judo trophies, and her well-worn paddock boots sat atop a stack of magazines. As she reached for the boots, she kicked off her cleats. One landed on a pile of clean clothes—oops!—but the other rolled through the closet door.

"Score!" Maddie mumbled, already yanking off her shirt. It was bright purple and had the logo of the Inner Bay Real Estate Pelicans printed on the front in silver. Most of Maddie's teammates considered their mascot kind of lame, but Maddie thought it was hilarious. Her family moved every few years because her mother was in the Air Force, which meant Maddie had played on four different local soccer teams since she was five years old. Two of them had been called the Tigers, and a third was the Lions. At least Pelicans was different!

Maddie paused at her dresser just long enough to glance in the mirror and check that her thick, wavy dark hair was still mostly contained in its ponytail. Then she grabbed her boots and sat down on the bed, almost squashing her laptop. That reminded her—she hadn't checked in on the Pony Post yet that day.

The Pony Post was a private message board dedicated to Chincoteague ponies—specifically, the ponies owned or ridden by the four members. The girls had never met in person, but they'd bonded online over their love of the special breed. It had been Maddie's idea to start the site, and for well over a year now the four of them had checked in daily and become fast friends.

Maddie flipped open the laptop. She hadn't had time to check in before soccer practice, so she couldn't resist logging on now, even though she was in a hurry. She'd posted several new photos of Cloudy the previous night, but due to the time difference—Maddie was on the West Coast, while the others lived in the Eastern or Central time zones—she knew her friends wouldn't have seen the pictures until that morning. It would only take a second to see if they'd posted yet. . . .

Maddie smiled as the familiar Pony Post logo popped up on the screen. Nina had designed it with help from her mom, who was a real-life artist. It showed four Chincoteague ponies galloping through the surf with the sun rising behind them. Below that were all four girls' names—Madison Martinez, Nina Peralt, Brooke Rhodes, and Haley Duncan. The rest of the screen provided space for the girls to share news, photos, and links. There were several new entries.

[BROOKE] Wow, I can't believe how much Cloudy looks like the original Misty of Chincoteague in that first pic!!

[NINA] I know, right? The only way u can tell it's not Misty is by looking at the background, lol. I keep expecting to see the waves of Chincoteague instead of the scenery of NorCal.

[HALEY] Great pix! Hey M, did u and Cloudy sign up yet for the Snack & Swim trail ride thing at your barn u were telling us about? It sounds like soooo much fun!

[NINA] Ya, and Cloudy will be fab at the swimming part! After all, she already swam across the channel to Chinc. when she was a baby.

[BROOKE] Just like the rest of our ponies. They would love that ride too! I wish we could all go!

[HALEY] Me too!

[NINA] Me three!

"Me four," Maddie said aloud. Clicking open a new text box, she got ready to type a response.

"Mads?" Her father's voice drifted upstairs. "You almost ready to go?"

Oops! Maddie realized that responding to her friends

would have to wait. If she didn't leave now, she'd be late for her lesson. And Ms. Emerson was pretty strict about stuff like that. Leaping up, Maddie rushed toward the door, figuring she could tie her boots in the car.

Maddie stared out the car window at the scenery flashing past, bright green lawns and landscaping vivid against the browns and yellows of native summer grasses. Normally she rode her bike to the barn, but it was a long ride, and on Saturdays she had both soccer practice and riding lessons, and not much time in between. Her dad was a part-time nurse at the local hospital, but when he wasn't working a weekend shift he usually drove her so she wouldn't have to rush through grooming and tacking up.

She was especially glad for the extra time today—and not only because Coach Wu had decided to throw in a few extra passing drills before she'd let them go. The comments from her Pony Post friends had reminded Maddie about the Snack & Swim, a group trail ride that ended in a bareback swim in a local creek and a picnic on the shore. The Snack & Swim ride was an annual event at Solano

Stables, but this would be Maddie's first year doing it. She'd wanted to go last year, but she'd only been riding Cloudy for about five months at the time and Ms. Emerson had decided the two of them weren't quite ready for that kind of adventure yet. But this year they were definitely ready, and Maddie couldn't wait.

"How's the team shaping up this summer?" Maddie's father asked, interrupting her thoughts of splashing into the cool water on Cloudy's round, warm back.

"Team?" Maddie turned and blinked at him. "What team?"

Her father grinned. "The U.S. Olympic Team," he joked. "What team do you think? I'm talking about the Pelicans!"

"Oh, soccer." Maddie shrugged. "It's fine, I guess. We won our first game last weekend, remember?"

"Hmm." Her father spun the wheel to take the turn onto the road leading to the stable. "You don't sound too excited. Don't tell me you're losing interest in soccer now."

Maddie couldn't help rolling her eyes. For some reason, her parents had decided she had a short attention span. Probably because she'd given up judo when she'd discovered riding—and realized it was more fun than anything else she'd ever done. What was the big deal about that? Other people were allowed to change their minds. Hadn't Tillie totally dropped her interest in ballet after discovering boys a couple of years ago? And one of her younger brothers, Tyler, seemed to come up with a new hobby every few weeks.

"Don't worry, I still like soccer," she assured her father.

"Good. Because you're terrific at it." He glanced over at her. "Besides, it's the type of activity you'll always be able to enjoy. It's easy to pick up anywhere in the country—or the world, for that matter."

Maddie shot him a surprised look, but he'd returned his gaze to the road. Why would he say something like that? Was it a hint? Did he think the Air Force was going to transfer Mom again? Maddie hoped not. After being there for more than two and a half years, Northern California felt like home. She had good friends there, she liked her school, and she'd probably make varsity basketball next year. And then there was Cloudy. . . .

Just then the familiar Solano Stables sign came into view up ahead. "Here we are," her father said. "Told you I'd get you here in plenty of time."

"Yeah." Maddie pushed her worries out of her mind. Why freak out about something that hadn't happened yet? "Thanks, Dad."

Maddie breathed in deeply as she hurried into Solano Stables. She loved the smell of the barn—a combination of horses, hay, leather, and fresh air.

The barn office was just inside the main entrance. Two of Maddie's friends were standing in front of the bulletin board by the door. Victoria and Valerie, better known as Vic and Val, were identical twins. They were also the reason Maddie had started riding. Vic had sat behind Maddie in fifth grade homeroom, and she'd spent so much time chattering about the riding lessons she and her sister had just started that Maddie had decided to give it a try—and the rest was history.

The twins both had wavy reddish-brown hair, though Val's was neatly pulled back in a ponytail while Vic's hung loose and wild. Vic was leaning forward, writing something on a sheet of paper hanging on the board while her twin watched.

"Stop!" Maddie exclaimed in mock dismay. "Neither of you better be signing up to take Cloudy on the Snack and Swim, or there's going to be trouble."

Vic giggled. "We wouldn't dare!"

"You don't have to worry," Val added. "Ms. Emerson wouldn't let anyone else sign up for Cloudy. She knows you've been looking forward to this all year."

"True," Vic agreed cheerfully. "And she knows you and Cloudy make an awesome team."

"We definitely do." A pen was hanging from the sign-up sheet by a piece of baling twine. Maddie grabbed it and scrawled her name below Vic's, along with Cloudy's. "There, now it's official."

"Cool." Vic lifted her hand for a high five. "The Snack and Swim is going to be epic!"

Meanwhile Val checked her watch. "We should start tacking up," she said. "Our lesson starts in thirteen minutes."

Maddie grinned. That was Val for you—she was very precise. "Okay, see you guys in the ring."

She ducked into the tack room beside the office to grab a brush and a hoof-pick, then took off toward Cloudy's stall. When she was a few doors away, she let out a short whistle. Immediately Cloudy's head poked out over her half door. The pony nickered, her ears up and framing the perfect white blaze running down her butterscotch-colored face.

Maddie's Pony Post friends were right—Cloudy really was the spitting image of Misty, the Chincoteague pony made world famous in the book *Misty of Chincoteague* by Marguerite Henry. That was why a local family had paid lots of money for Cloudy as a foal almost ten years ago at the annual Chincoteague wild pony auction and then spent even more to ship her all the way out to California.

Unfortunately, they hadn't really known what to do with the spunky little weanling once she got there. Over the next few years, Cloudy had grown older and wilder as the family's kids had "trained" her by trial and (mostly) error. After getting kicked out of yet another local barn when the now eight-year-old and still unruly Cloudy had knocked down one of the barn workers, the perplexed and fed-up parents had offered to sell the pony cheap to Ms. Emerson. The barn owner had had her doubts, but she believed in giving every horse a chance. So she'd bought Cloudy and brought her to Solano Stables.

And to her surprise, Ms. Emerson had discovered that beneath the lack of discipline, the little pinto mare actually had a nice, willing temperament. A month or two of training later, Cloudy was already being used in lessons by advanced students. And a couple of months after that, Maddie—who had been intrigued with Cloudy since the mare's arrival—asked if she could give the pony a try. Ms. Emerson had been dubious, since Maddie had only been taking lessons for a few months at that point. But Maddie had talked her into it, and she and Cloudy had quickly become a great team.

Almost a year and a half later, the mare was now a reliable school horse, popular with beginners and experienced riders alike. But Maddie was pretty sure Cloudy loved her best!

"Hey, girl," she said, letting herself into the stall. "What's up?"

Cloudy nickered again, nudging at Maddie's arm with her soft nose. Maddie smiled and dug a peppermint horse treat out of her pocket.

"Just one for now," she said as the pony carefully lipped the treat off her palm. "We have to hurry and get ready. Good thing you're pretty clean today."

As she started grooming the pony, Maddie heard the twins calling her name from the aisle. She poked her head out of the stall.

"What's the matter?" she asked, noting their worried faces. That wasn't so unusual for Val—she was often worried about something or other. But Vic looked anxious too.

"We just noticed something," Val said breathlessly. "We were looking at the lesson list to see who we're riding today . . ."

Maddie nodded. Ms. Emerson posted a list on the

bulletin board with the day's horse assignments, though Maddie never bothered to check it anymore. She always rode Cloudy.

Vic finished her twin's sentence: ". . . and we thought we were seeing things," she said. "Because you're not assigned to ride Cloudy today—Ms. Emerson wrote you down to ride Wizard instead!"

◆ CHAPTER ◆
2

"THAT'S WEIRD," MADDIE SAID. "CLOUDY isn't lame or anything. Why wouldn't I be riding her? Especially with the Snack and Swim coming up so soon." She shrugged and let herself out of the stall. "It's probably a mistake. I'll go find out."

"Yeah, it's got to be a mistake." Vic nodded, seeming satisfied, though Val still looked concerned.

Maddie hurried back up the aisle to the bulletin board. Sure enough, there was her name on the lesson list—with Wizard's name written beside it in Ms. Emerson's tidy handwriting.

"Weird," Maddie murmured. Ms. Emerson didn't

usually make mistakes like that. She was the most capable and practical person Maddie knew. Even the barn owner's short brown hair seemed designed for maximum efficiency!

Maddie heard voices outside the main doors. As she glanced over, Ms. Emerson stepped into view, accompanied by a tall, lanky blond woman Maddie had never seen before. The woman looked a little older than Maddie's mom; she was dressed in shorts, sandals, and a sleeveless polo shirt, with a pair of sunglasses perched on her head. She looked tanned, fit, and sporty, like many of the women at the country club where Maddie and her brothers took swimming lessons.

". . . and this is the main barn," Ms. Emerson was saying.

"Lovely." The woman glanced around and smiled. "It's very tidy, isn't it?"

Maddie was dying to rush right over and ask the barn owner about the lesson list. But she didn't dare interrupt, and not only because Ms. Emerson would probably be annoyed. Maddie's military mom had done her best to instill good manners in all four of her children, and that early training usually overrode Maddie's natural impulsiveness. Usually. Though in this case, Maddie was tempted to make an exception. . . .

As Ms. Emerson led the other woman toward the office, the two of them started chatting about lesson prices and available times. Maddie figured the blond woman was just another lesson mom signing her kids up for riding. It wouldn't be a big deal to break in and ask Ms. Emerson about Cloudy, would it?

Just then Ms. Emerson noticed Maddie. "Madison," she said in her no-nonsense voice. "Why are you just standing there? Don't you have a lesson in"—she checked her watch—"less than ten minutes?"

"Um, that's what I wanted to ask you about," Maddie said. "I saw that you put me on the list next to Wizard—"

The stable owner cut her off briskly. "That's right. And the last time I saw him, he had a big manure stain on his shoulder. So you'd better do some fast grooming."

Maddie bit her lip. "Um, but what about Cloudy? I just thought—"

Once again the stable owner didn't let her finish. "Cloudy is doing a private lesson later," she said. "Today you're assigned to ride Wizard."

Maddie nodded. She wasn't afraid to speak her mind, even with adults. But she didn't quite dare question Ms. Emerson further when the riding teacher used that tone of voice. Besides, Ms. Emerson wasn't paying attention to her anymore. She was busy ushering the blond woman into the office.

Maddie's head was spinning as she hurried back to Cloudy's stall to collect her grooming tools. "Sorry, girl," she said, giving the mare a pat. "Guess I won't be riding you today after all."

She couldn't help being disappointed. Maddie loved all horses and ponies, but she and Cloudy had clicked in a special way that hadn't happened with any of the others.

Back out in the aisle, Maddie had to stop for a second to remember where her assigned mount's stall was. Wizard was a fat gray pony with a perpetually tousled mane and a placid temperament. Maddie had ridden him a few times when she was first starting out, and occasionally one of the twins still drew his name for a lesson. But most of the time Ms. Emerson saved him for timid riders or brand-new beginners.

Wizard was eating hay in his stall when Maddie peeked in. As soon as she saw him, she let out a groan. Ms. Emerson hadn't been kidding about that manure stain!

"Get ready, boy," she warned the pony as she let herself into his stall. "This is going to be the world's fastest grooming."

Less than ten minutes later, Maddie was leading Wizard into the stable's outdoor arena, a large, sandy oval with shade trees lining one long side and a set of bleachers along the other. Beyond the bleachers, hills undulated toward the bright blue sky, some of them striped with a vineyard's orderly rows of grapevines. But Maddie didn't look in that direction—instead, she glanced at the far end of the ring, past which the land sloped down to the start of the public trail leading through acres of irrigated fields and eventually to a local park. That was where the Snack & Swim ride would take place. She couldn't wait!

The twins were over near the mounting block. Val was

tightening her mount's girth, while Vic played with her pony's long forelock. Maddie led Wizard toward them.

"Wow." Vic's eyes widened as she glanced up. "It's so weird to see you with a different horse!"

"I know, right?" Maddie glanced at Wizard, who was plodding along sleepily behind her. She'd managed to get most of the manure stain off, though his shoulder still had a slight greenish tinge. "I haven't ridden Wiz in forever."

Val looped her reins over her arm and tightened the chin strap of her helmet. "You haven't ridden anyone but Cloudy in forever," she said.

"Yeah, pretty much." Maddie glanced at the gate, surprised that Ms. Emerson wasn't there yet. "I mean, there've been a couple of times when she had an abscess or a snotty nose or something."

"And then there was the time she missed a whole week's worth of lessons when that car company leased her to be in their TV commercial, remember?" Vic said.

Maddie nodded. "But I knew about that ahead of time."

"So what's going on? Is Cloudy sick or something?" Val looked worried.

"No," Maddie replied. "Ms. Emerson said she's doing a private lesson later. I didn't get to ask her about it, though, because she was giving some lady a tour, and—"

"Shh." Vic shot a warning look at the gate.

Ms. Emerson strode in. "Ready to go, girls?" she asked. "Let's mount up."

"Can you check my girth?" Val asked. "I tried to tighten it, but Susie keeps stomping her foot."

As the barn owner stepped over to help Val, Maddie checked Wizard's girth and pulled down the stirrups on the saddle. "Come on, boy," she said with a cluck. "Time to get going."

She led the pony over to the mounting block and swung aboard. Even though Wizard *looked* round, his back felt narrower than Cloudy's, and at first Maddie couldn't quite figure out where to let her legs hang. She was fiddling with her stirrups when Ms. Emerson walked over.

"Everything all right, Maddie?" she asked, sliding a hand under Wizard's girth to make sure it was tight enough.

"I think so." Maddie stuck her foot back in the stirrup. "He just feels . . . different. I'm used to Cloudy, I guess."

She shot Ms. Emerson a sidelong look, hoping the barn owner might provide some further explanation for why Maddie wasn't riding Cloudy today. But Ms. Emerson just gave Wizard a pat and then stepped back. "All right, girls," she said to all three of them. "Let's get started. Take the rail to the right, please."

Maddie gave Wizard a nudge with her legs. The pony didn't move, so she kicked a little harder.

"Come on, buddy," she muttered. "Let's go."

Wizard finally creaked into a walk, and Maddie aimed him at a spot on the rail in front of Vic's pony. She and Cloudy almost always led the way in their lessons. Even though the Chincoteague pony wasn't very tall, she walked faster than any of the other lesson ponies and even most of the horses.

But Maddie wasn't riding Cloudy today. She was riding Wizard, and he definitely wasn't one of the faster ponies in the barn. Within seconds, Vic's pony was practically on Wizard's heels.

"Easy!" Ms. Emerson called out. "Be careful how close you're getting, Victoria."

"Sorry!" Vic called back. She circled her pony, ending up behind her twin's mount.

"Come on, Wiz," Maddie said, giving her pony another solid kick. "Let's pick up the pace."

The gray pony lifted his head and stepped out a little faster—but only for a few strides. Then he settled back to his usual speed.

"Look out!" Val called out. "Passing on the right, okay?"

"Me too," Vic said.

Soon both of them were in front of Maddie. Even then Maddie had trouble keeping Wizard moving. She had to nudge or kick or cluck at almost every stride.

This is a lot more work than riding Cloudy! she thought as she kicked again, trying to keep up with the others.

"All right, let's get ready to pick up a trot," Ms. Emerson said after a few minutes.

Maddie immediately tightened her grip on the reins. Whenever Cloudy heard the word "trot," she surged forward into the faster gait without waiting for her rider's cue.

But once again, Maddie was reminded that Wizard wasn't Cloudy when the gray gelding halted. "Oops," she muttered, kicking him on again and loosening her reins.

"Go ahead and trot when you're ready," Ms. Emerson said. "All the way around, then circle at the far end. Remember to ask for a proper bend. . . ."

There were more instructions, but Maddie wasn't really listening. Most of her attention was focused on trying to get Wizard to trot. The twins' ponies were both halfway down the next long side before the little gray managed a lumbering trot. Maddie started posting, closing her legs on his sides on each downbeat as she'd been taught. Even so, Wizard soon lost energy and broke back to a walk.

"Keep trotting, Maddie," Ms. Emerson called out.

"I know. He's being super-lazy!" Maddie exclaimed, giving the gray pony a firm kick with both heels. "Come *on*, Wiz!"

"Easy with your leg," Ms. Emerson said.

"But he's not listening!" Maddie slumped in the saddle and the pony drifted back to a walk and then a halt. "I'm used to Cloudy—she always wants to go."

"Come back to walk, please," Ms. Emerson called to the twins. Then she turned to Maddie. "You can't get frustrated with a pony just because he's not like another pony. That's not fair."

"Sorry." Maddie frowned and glanced down at Wizard. "He's just really different. He doesn't want to go at all."

"That's exactly why I assigned you to him. He's been extra poky with the tiny beginners lately, and he needs someone strong enough to remind him how to respond properly to the aids."

"Oh." Maddie felt a twinge of pride that the barn owner thought she was a good enough rider to help keep the pony schooled for beginners. "Okay. But I wish I had a crop."

"If you really can't keep him moving, I'll go get you one. But first I'd like you to try again without."

"Okay." Maddie gathered up her reins. "Here we go, Wiz. Trot on!"

She gave the pony a firm squeeze with both legs. "Shoulders back and eyes forward," Ms. Emerson said. "There you go!"

Maddie smiled. "Good boy!" she told Wizard as he

picked up a trot. It still wasn't very fast, and it wasn't nearly as smooth as Cloudy's trot. But this time she managed to keep him going until Ms. Emerson called for a walk.

"Thanks, boy," Maddie said, running a brush over Wizard's back to rub out the sweat mark the saddle had left on his gray coat. "That was . . . interesting."

She grimaced, thinking back over the lesson. It definitely hadn't been her best. Maddie had ridden better after Ms. Emerson's little talk, but Wizard had remained lazy the entire time. It had taken Maddie three tries to get him to canter, and when it was time to jump, she'd held her breath over every tiny crossrail, half afraid the poky pony might not manage the energy to heave himself to the other side. All the way through, Maddie couldn't help thinking about how much better Cloudy would have done at everything and how much more fun she was to ride.

But that wasn't really fair, Maddie reminded herself. Okay, so Wizard wasn't Cloudy. But he was definitely an amazing pony in his own way. He was so steady and sweet that even the most frightened beginner felt safe on him.

He'd taught lots of kids to be confident enough to move on to more challenging mounts. As Ms. Emerson often said, he was worth his weight in gold.

"You're a good boy, aren't you?" Maddie murmured, digging into the pony's white mane to give his crest a scratch. Wizard stretched his neck out, his lower lip flopping and his eyes half closed. Maddie smiled. "You like that, huh?"

She heard footsteps in the aisle and stepped to the door to see if they belonged to the twins. Instead she saw Kiana, who was in her early twenties and a native of Hawaii. Kiana had moved to Northern California to attend one of the local universities, and she helped Ms. Emerson run the barn part-time during the school year and full-time in the summer. At the moment her straight, fine black hair was flopping out of her ponytail as usual, and she was carrying a broom.

"Hi, Maddie." As usual, Kiana's smile was wide and friendly. "Have a good lesson today?"

"Sort of," Maddie said. With a slightly guilty glance at Wizard, she added, "I mean yeah, definitely. But listen, I was just wondering—do you know why Ms. E is giving some private lesson on Cloudy today?"

Kiana pushed a strand of hair out of her round dark eyes. "Oh, you mean the Richardson thing? Is that today?"

"Richardson thing?" Maddie didn't know anyone named Richardson. "Is that a new lesson student or something? Oh! Maybe it's got to do with that tall blond lady I saw with Ms. E earlier."

Kiana blinked at her. "Yeah, that was probably Mrs. Richardson. She just got back here with some of the kids, I think."

"Kids?" Maddie was feeling more confused by the second. "What kids?"

"The Richardson kids." Kiana shifted the broom to her other hand and gazed at Maddie. "Wait, I thought you knew about all this."

"All what?"

"The Richardsons." Kiana shrugged. "They're the family that sold Cloudy to us—the ones who bought her out east at the pony auction. They heard how well she's been doing lately, and now they might be interested in buying her back."

✦ CHAPTER ✦

3

"WHAT?" MADDIE COULDN'T BELIEVE HER ears. "What do you mean, they want to buy her back? Cloudy can't leave!"

"I'm with you." Kiana sounded sympathetic. "Cloudy's one of our best lesson ponies. But it's up to Ms. E, I guess. She's the boss, right?"

"But she can't sell Cloudy!" Maddie clutched the top of the stall door so tightly, her knuckles turned white. "Anyway, why would those people want her back? They're the ones who almost ruined her!"

Kiana shook her head. "Sorry, sweetie, I don't know

much more than what I just told you. You'll need to ask Ms. E about the details."

"I will." Maddie let herself out of the stall and rushed down the aisle.

Halfway to the office, she almost crashed into Val, who was stepping out of a stall. "Whoa!" Vic said, emerging behind her twin. "Where are you going?"

"To talk to Ms. Emerson." Maddie took a deep breath. "You'll never believe this. . . ."

She quickly filled her friends in on what Kiana had told her. By the time she finished, both twins looked just as dismayed as Maddie felt.

"Oh my gosh! This is terrible!" Vic exclaimed.

"Cloudy can't leave." Val twisted her hands together the way she did when she was feeling especially anxious. "And she definitely can't go back to her old owners."

"No kidding." Maddie grimaced as she thought back to Cloudy's early days at Solano Stables. The mare had been so unruly that Ms. Emerson hadn't even let anyone else lead her out to the pasture at first, let alone ride her. "They obviously didn't know anything about training horses. They'd probably just let Cloudy run wild again!"

"Yeah," Vic said. "It would be crazy to send her back to them."

"So why is Ms. E considering it?" Maddie wondered. "She's not usually—"

"Oops, Mom's here." Val waved at her mother, who had just appeared in the doorway at the end of the aisle. "We've got to go."

"Yeah. But text us later and let us know what Ms. Emerson says, okay?" Vic added, following her sister up the aisle.

"I will," Maddie said.

She continued on to the office, but it was deserted. That was no surprise. As the owner and head instructor of a busy lesson barn, Ms. Emerson rarely sat still for long.

Maddie kept searching. As she wandered down the main aisle, she saw Cloudy coming out of her stall, wearing saddle and bridle and led by a girl Maddie didn't know. The girl looked a couple of years older than Maddie, tall for her age, with the same pale blond hair and lanky build as the woman Maddie had seen earlier.

Maddie's heart raced. The girl didn't seem to notice her standing there, staring, as she led Cloudy out of the barn in the direction of the outdoor ring.

That's got to be one of the Richardson kids, Maddie thought.

She hurried after girl and pony, emerging just in time to see the girl lead Cloudy into the ring. The blond woman—Mrs. Richardson, Maddie knew now—was sitting in the bleachers, fiddling with her smartphone. A blond girl who looked to be maybe eight or nine years old was perched beside her, while two other kids—a boy about the same age and a younger girl—chased each other around in the grass nearby.

But most of Maddie's attention was on the girl with Cloudy. Ms. Emerson was already helping her adjust her girth and stirrups.

"All right, shall we mount up?" The barn owner's voice didn't seem that loud, but it carried easily to where Maddie was standing, in the shadow of the barn overhang. "Lead Cloudy over to the block."

"I don't need a mounting block." The blond girl's voice was confident. "We used to get on from the ground all the time when we had her. I could always get on, even though I was a lot shorter back then."

"I understand. But here we always use a mounting block." Ms. Emerson's voice was kind but firm. "It's better for the horses' backs, and better for the tack as well."

"Oh." The girl sounded dubious. "Okay, whatever."

She hopped onto the block as Ms. Emerson positioned Cloudy beside it. Soon the girl was in the saddle.

"Looking good, Amber!" Mrs. Richardson called out, glancing up briefly from her phone.

The girl—Amber—didn't respond. She picked up the reins so quickly and firmly that Cloudy tossed her head and took a step backward.

"Easy with your hands," Ms. Emerson said. "Let's start out with a walk around on the rail so you and Cloudy can get to know each other."

"We already know each other, remember?" Amber said. She gave Cloudy a thump with both legs, sending the startled mare spurting forward at a trot.

"Walk, please," Ms. Emerson said firmly.

Maddie guessed the command was as much for

Cloudy's benefit as the rider's. The mare was smart—she knew lots of words. Obeying the instructor's command, she slowed to a brisk walk.

"All right, let's talk about this," Ms. Emerson said. "Keep her on a circle around me."

Amber nodded and yanked on one rein. Maddie winced as Cloudy put her ears flat back and swished her tail, stopping short.

"Giddyup, Cloudy," Amber ordered, giving another kick to start the mare walking again.

Cloudy jumped forward, but this time she stayed at a walk. Her head was cranked around to one side, and she didn't look happy. But she went the way the girl was pulling, walking around Ms. Emerson in a tight circle.

"Cloudy might feel a little different than you remember, Amber." Ms. Emerson's voice was calm, much calmer than Maddie felt as she watched Amber continue to yank and kick Cloudy around the circle. "She's been working as a lesson pony for a while now, and she knows all the cues we use to ask her to do things. We call those cues the aids. Are you familiar with that term?"

Amber frowned. "Um . . ."

"She means like using your legs to make Cloudy go!" a high-pitched voice called from the bleachers.

Maddie glanced that way. The nine-year-old girl was standing by the rail now, watching the lesson intently.

"Shut up, Felicia," Amber called.

"Language, Amber." Mrs. Richardson looked up from her phone. "Watch it, or the lesson is over."

"Sorry, Mom." Amber waited until her mother looked down again, then rolled her eyes.

"Your sister is correct," Ms. Emerson told Amber. "There are a variety of aids, broken into two categories— natural and artificial. Your leg is one of the natural aids. Can you guess what the rest might be?"

"I'm not sure." Amber gave another yank on the rein as Cloudy started to drift out. "The other leg? No, wait—how about the reins?"

"Close. Your hands would be considered another natural aid," Ms. Emerson replied. "Speaking of which, be careful about the way you're pulling. Try more of a gentle give-and-take motion when you want her to turn."

Amber glanced down and loosened the reins slightly. "Are we going to trot soon?"

"In a moment." Ms. Emerson turned to the viewers by the bleachers. "Felicia, can you tell me the other two natural aids?"

"Seat and voice," the younger girl piped up immediately.

"That's right." Ms. Emerson sounded pleased and slightly surprised. She smiled at Felicia, then turned her attention back to Amber, talking to her about proper use of the aids.

I hope Amber's listening, Maddie thought, gritting her teeth as Cloudy shook her head against the reins. *Because Cloudy doesn't look very happy about the way she's riding.*

The lesson continued. Amber was obviously confident in the saddle, and after a few reminders she loosened up on the reins and stopped kicking so hard—at least most of the time. Maddie found herself wondering if this was the first real riding lesson the girl had ever had. If her siblings rode the same way, it was no wonder Cloudy had arrived at Solano Stables unschooled and confused!

Amber wasn't bad at posting the trot, though she had no idea what a diagonal was and seemed unimpressed with the whole concept of rising and sitting according to which direction she was going. Maddie guessed that meant she probably didn't know anything about proper canter leads either, though luckily Cloudy was a pro and picked it up correctly the first time in both directions.

"All right, bring her down," Ms. Emerson said after Amber and Cloudy's second canter circuit of the ring. "Very nice. I think we'll end there."

Amber pulled the mare to a halt. "Wait, can't we try jumping?" she asked, glancing at the pair of crossrails set up on the quarter line. "I know Cloudy knows how—my older sister and brother used to jump her over stuff all the time."

"No, we'll leave jumping for another day," Ms. Emerson said.

"But I know I could do it!" Amber protested.

"Another day." The instructor's voice was firm. "I'll hold Cloudy while you dismount."

Maddie held her breath, afraid the older girl was about to roll her eyes again. Ms. Emerson might have tolerated that when it was aimed at Amber's mother, but Maddie knew from personal experience that the barn owner had no patience for that sort of thing being directed at herself.

Luckily for Amber, she just sighed. "Okay, fine," she said.

"What do you say to Ms. Emerson, Amber?" Mrs. Richardson called from the bleachers as Amber swung down from the saddle.

"Thank you," Amber said. "It was a pretty fun lesson, I guess. And Cloudy was great!"

On that point Maddie had to agree. She'd seen Cloudy give beginner lessons before. But usually the new riders were too busy trying to figure out how to keep all their body parts where they were supposed to be to bother the horse much. Maddie was surprised that Ms. Emerson hadn't put Amber on a lunge line, as she often did while teaching newbies not to yank or balance on the reins.

Ms. Emerson showed Amber how to run up her stirrups to keep them from banging on the pony's sides, then opened the gate. Felicia ran over and started chattering eagerly at the barn owner, asking all kinds of questions about the lesson she'd just seen. Meanwhile Amber led Cloudy out of the ring, with her mother and the other two siblings trailing along behind them. Maddie couldn't resist stepping out of the shadows as the whole group moved toward her.

"Hi," she said. "I'm Maddie. I take lessons here, too—I ride Cloudy a lot, actually."

"Really? Cool." Amber's smile was a little distant, probably due to the difference in their ages, but she sounded friendly enough. "Cloudy's awesome, isn't she?"

"It's nice to meet you, Maddie," Mrs. Richardson added with a smile. "You must be a good rider—I can't imagine our Cloudy would be doing so well otherwise."

Maddie winced at that term—"our Cloudy." *She's not yours!* she wanted to yell. *Not anymore.*

Instead she just said, "Thanks. Cloudy's taught me a lot." She reached out to stroke the mare's nose. Cloudy nickered and nudged her, clearly hoping for a treat, but Amber pulled the pony's head away.

"We actually used to own Cloudy, you know." Amber waved vaguely in the direction of her family. "I helped my older sister and brother put the basics on her when she was young." She gave the mare a pat on the neck. "Guess we did a pretty good job, huh? 'Cause look at her now!"

Maddie forced a smile. "Um, yeah. Cloudy's great."

Mrs. Richardson glanced at her smartphone, looking distracted. "Yes, we heard through the grapevine that Cloudy ended up being one of this stable's most reliable lesson horses. Now that the younger kids are showing an interest in riding, we decided to look into buying her back." She glanced at the youngest girl and the boy, who appeared to be squabbling over a rock they were kicking around on the path behind them. "Frank! Baby!" she added sharply. "Cut it out!"

She hurried off toward the kids. Left alone with Amber, Maddie shot the older girl a sidelong look. "So, um, you're getting back into riding?" she asked.

"Sort of." Cloudy had drifted to a stop and stretched her head toward a patch of weeds. Amber tugged on the reins to get her moving again. "It's mostly Felicia, though. She took a lesson at her friend's barn, and now she's horse crazy." She rolled her eyes. "Never stops blabbing about it, actually. She was only like six or seven when we sold

Cloudy, so she never got to ride much back then. Especially since Cloudy was a total brat at our last barn. Nobody but Raina—that's my older sister—could even handle her most of the time, so Mom and Dad kept the younger ones away. That's why they sold her when Raina went to college."

Maddie winced, flashing back again to how spoiled and willful Cloudy had been during her first few days at Solano Stables. "Oh, really?" she said, afraid that if she said anything else, she'd end up telling Amber that it was her family's fault that Cloudy had ended up that way.

"Uh-huh. Raina says the barn owner there didn't know what she was doing. She fed Cloudy this really cheap sweet feed, and it made her nuts."

Maddie bit her lip, hearing her mother's voice in her head saying, *If you can't say anything nice, don't say anything at all.*

"Um, okay . . . ," she mumbled.

Just then Ms. Emerson and Felicia caught up to them. "Why don't you take Cloudy back to her stall," the barn owner told Amber. "Do you remember how to untack?"

"I know how!" Felicia piped in brightly.

Amber shot her sister a slightly sour look. "Don't worry,

I've got it." She gave another tug on the reins. "Come on, Cloudy. Let's go."

They disappeared into the barn, with Felicia right behind them. Maddie was about to follow when Ms. Emerson put a hand on her arm.

"Hold up a second, Maddie." The barn owner glanced at Mrs. Richardson, but the woman was still busy scolding her two younger kids back by the ring. "I want to talk to you—I hope you're not too upset about this Cloudy situation."

Of course I'm upset! Maddie wanted to shout. Instead, she just nodded and waited to see what Ms. Emerson would say next.

"I want you to understand, this is all very preliminary at this point," Ms. Emerson went on. "The Richardsons haven't decided they definitely want to buy Cloudy back. They're just exploring the idea. I've agreed to give the kids a few lessons to let them test the waters."

"Oh," Maddie choked out. That didn't sound very preliminary to her. Once Amber and Felicia rode Cloudy a few times, how could they help falling in love with her? Especially Felicia, if she was as horse crazy as her sister said.

Ms. Emerson was watching her carefully. "I mean it, Maddie," she said. "You shouldn't panic or assume Cloudy will be leaving us."

"Okay." Maddie wasn't sure what else to say. Then she remembered something. "Um, the Snack and Swim—"

"Oh yes, I meant to mention that." Ms. Emerson smiled. "You don't have to worry. Cloudy will definitely be here for the big ride next weekend, and nobody will ride her except you that day. I promise."

Maddie nodded. Ms. Emerson never made promises she couldn't keep.

Still, that didn't make her feel much better. Okay, so she'd get to ride Cloudy for the Snack & Swim. What about after that? What if the Richardsons did decide to buy their pony back and take her away?

What would Maddie do if she lost Cloudy?

"Ew, what's this doing on my bed?"

Maddie glanced up from her desk. Tillie was glaring at her from her half of the room, holding Maddie's soccer shirt between one thumb and forefinger as if it might be some kind of potential biohazard.

"Oh. Sorry." Maddie shrugged and hit send on her phone. It was half an hour after dinner, and she'd just finished texting the twins about what had happened after they'd left the stable earlier that day. "Just throw it in the hamper."

Tillie tossed the shirt onto Maddie's rumpled bed. "*You* throw it in the hamper. I don't want to smell like tween tomboy sweat tonight." She stepped over to her tidy dresser and picked up a tube of lip gloss.

"Whatever," Maddie muttered. Then she thought of something. "Hey, Till, do you know a girl named Amber Richardson? I think she's around your age."

"I don't think so." Tillie slicked on a coat of cranberry-colored lip gloss, then smacked her lips together. "Wait, yes I do. Blond, kind of pushy?"

"That sounds right, yeah."

Tillie glanced at Maddie in the mirror. "She's a year behind me. She tried out for cheerleading last year when I was cocaptain of the middle school squad, but then she quit to play tennis or something instead. Why?"

"Just curious." Maddie kept her tone casual. "She came to the barn today."

"Oh." Tillie immediately lost interest and returned her attention to her primping.

Dropping the phone on her desk, Maddie heaved herself to her feet. As she grabbed the dirty T-shirt off her bed, she noticed the corner of her laptop peeking out from under the bedsheet. Suddenly she remembered she'd never logged back on to the Pony Post. She'd been too distracted by her worries about Cloudy—the Richardson Situation, as she'd started calling it in her head—to think about anything else.

She flopped onto the bed and flipped open the laptop. When she logged on, there were several new messages.

[NINA] Went for a ride along the levee today after my lesson. It was perfection! Breezy was amazing and chill, even when we passed a whole herd of bikes. Such a good boy!

[BROOKE] Breezy is always amazing! lol! Glad u had fun! Foxy and I just messed around at home today. It was 2 hot to do much, so I just hopped on bareback and we practiced some dressage stuff or whatev.

[NINA] Bareback dressage? Awesome! U and Foxy should enter a show sometime—it sounds like you're getting rly good.

[BROOKE] Maybe if I can save enough $. But I dunno if we're good enough.

[HALEY] Hi guys! B, you are totally good enough to show.

[NINA] Hi H! Did u ride today?

[HALEY] Of course! I want to make sure Wings is fit enough for our jumping lesson next week. Can't wait!

[HALEY] btw, where's Maddie? She hasn't checked in since she posted those pix last night.

[BROOKE] I'm sure she'll post soon. She's probably still at the barn having fun w/Cloudy.

[NINA] Or maybe she ran into a famous movie star on her way home and got whisked off to a big film premiere or something, lol!

Maddie grinned at Nina's post. Maddie's Pony Post friends seemed to think the entire state of California was crawling with movie stars and other celebrities, no matter how many times she tried to tell them that Hollywood was like an eight-hour drive away.

Her smile faded as she came back to reality. How was she going to break the news to her Pony Post friends about the Richardson Situation?

She scanned their posts again, lingering over the details about the fun they'd all had with their Chincoteague ponies that day. *Their* ponies. That was the key word, wasn't it? Nina and Brooke owned their ponies, and Haley's was free leased from an elderly neighbor who had said she could keep him as long as she liked. That meant they didn't have to worry about having their ponies snatched out from under them.

Until today, Maddie hadn't worried about that either. She'd taken for granted that Cloudy would be at Solano Stables forever. It was still almost impossible to believe that that might not be true. . . .

"What's with you?" Tillie asked, stopping beside Maddie's bed on her way to the closet. "You look all angsty."

"Nothing." Maddie quickly signed off and closed her laptop. "Just checking messages and stuff, that's all."

Tillie shrugged, grabbed a pair of shoes off the organized rack in her half of the closet, and hurried out of the room. Maddie just sat there for a moment, feeling vaguely guilty for not telling her friends what was going on.

Then again, Cloudy wasn't gone yet. The Richardsons had given up on her once—maybe they'd do it again.

So until Maddie knew anything for sure, why upset her Pony Post friends over something that might not even happen?

◆ CHAPTER ◆
4

"ALL ABOARD FOR FOG CITY!" MADDIE'S father sang out as he strode into the kitchen the next morning.

Maddie was sitting on the bench by the back door, tying her sneakers. "I'm ready. But you'll have to tell Ry and Ty there's no time for a third helping of cereal."

"Shut up, I'm finished." Maddie's youngest brother, nine-year-old Tyler, dumped his bowl in the sink with a clatter. He patted his skinny belly. "Anyway, I'm saving my appetite for steamed buns."

Ryan didn't bother to answer. He just kept shoveling cereal into his mouth while reading the back of the box.

Tillie yawned as she put the orange juice carton back in the fridge. "I still don't see why we have to leave so early. It's the weekend, you know!"

Her mother bustled in just in time to hear her. "We want to be there when the museum opens," she said. "We've got a busy day planned."

Maddie nodded, feeling a surge of excitement. Her parents both had unpredictable work schedules, and it wasn't often that the entire family got the chance to spend a whole day together. But this was one of those rare occasions. They were planning to drive into nearby San Francisco and spend the morning at the Exploratorium, then head over to their favorite dim sum place in China-town, followed by shopping at Union Square—the latter being the only way Tillie would agree to the rest without complaining.

"Okay, I'm finished," Ryan announced a moment later. He set his bowl in the sink with the others and pushed his glasses up his nose. "Whose turn is it to load the dish-washer?"

"Leave the dishes—I'll do them when we get home."

Mr. Martinez checked his watch. "Let's hit the road."

Maddie was heading for the door when the phone rang. Her mother grabbed it. "Hello?" She listened for a moment, then held out the receiver. "Maddie, it's for you."

Maddie froze. Who would be calling her at this hour on a Sunday morning? Her mind immediately jumped to Cloudy. Had the Richardsons already made up their minds? Was Ms. Emerson calling to tell Maddie she'd have to find another mount for the Snack & Swim ride after all?

"Um, who is it?" Maddie asked, trying not to sound as panicky as she felt.

"Coach Wu," her mother replied. "Make it quick, okay? We need to get going."

Maddie nodded, relief flooding through her. She had no idea why her soccer coach was calling, but she was pretty sure it had nothing to do with Cloudy.

"Hello?" she said.

"Maddie? Hope I didn't call too early." Coach Wu's voice sounded excited. "Didn't want to miss you. Got a minute?"

"I guess so." Maddie shot a look at her family. They were all hovering near the door, staring at her. "What's up?"

"Big news. I just found out you've been invited to try out for the Cascade League!"

Maddie gasped. "Are you kidding me?" The Cascade League was the most competitive travel league in Northern California. Maddie had gone to watch a couple of their local games, and the players were super-intense.

Coach Wu laughed. "I wouldn't kid about this. Congratulations, Maddie! And congratulations to me, too." She sounded pleased. "This is the first time since I took over as head coach that one of my players has been invited to try out."

"Wow." Maddie leaned against the wall, stunned. "This is awesome."

"Yeah. Anyway, I just wanted to let you know right away. We can talk details at practice on Tuesday."

"What was that about?" Tillie asked as Maddie hung up.

Maddie explained as the family headed out and climbed into the minivan. ". . . and a Pelican hasn't been asked to try out in like three years," she finished as she clicked on her seat belt. "It's super-selective, and only the most promising kids from all the local leagues get scouted."

"Excellent." Her father glanced at her in the rearview mirror, sounding proud. "This could open lots of doors for you, Mads."

"Thanks, Dad." Maddie leaned back against her seat. "But don't get your hopes up, okay? I mean, there's no guarantee I'll make the team on my first try—"

"Yeah, you probably won't," Tyler put in with a smirk.

"But even being asked to try out is, like, a huge honor," Maddie finished, ignoring her brother. "This is really cool."

As Mr. Martinez pulled the car out of the driveway, Sergeant Martinez turned around in her seat to talk to Maddie. "So what's involved in this Cascade League if you do make it?" she asked. "It won't interfere with school, will it?"

"It's just for the summer. I think." Maddie shrugged. "Actually, I'm not sure. I never really thought I'd get invited to try out, so I never paid that much attention."

"I'll look it up if you want," Tillie volunteered. She fished her new smartphone out of her purse. She'd saved up for more than six months to buy it and never missed a chance to show it off—or so it seemed to Maddie.

It didn't take long for Tillie to bring up the Cascade League's official website. She scanned it.

"Well? What's it say?" Tyler demanded from the backseat. He was leaning forward, straining against his seat belt. Beside him, Ryan already had his nose buried in a comic book. He didn't appear to be paying attention, though Maddie knew her quiet ten-year-old brother heard more than people thought.

"It sounds pretty hard-core," Tillie said, scrolling down. "You practice at least four times a week, plus you have to go to these special coaching seminars and stuff. And then of course you travel to the games every weekend."

"What kind of travel are we talking about?" Mr. Martinez asked.

Tillie was still scrolling. "Well, for the junior league—that's what Maddie would be trying out for—the regular games are supposed to stay within seventy miles of your team's home base—"

"Seventy miles?" Maddie broke in. "Whoa, that's far."

"Yeah. But then it sounds like the championships can be even farther away than that, and some of the coaching thingies too."

"Wow," Maddie's mother said. "Sounds like a serious time commitment."

Mr. Martinez nodded, glancing at Maddie in the rearview again. "Yeah. You'd probably have to drop your other activities for a while—including riding."

"What?" Okay, that changed things. Suddenly Maddie wasn't feeling so excited anymore. "Forget it. Riding is way more important to me than some soccer team. I'll call Coach Wu later and have her tell the Cascade League thanks, but no thanks."

In the front seat, her parents traded a look. "Don't make any hasty decisions, Maddie," her mother warned. "This could be a great opportunity for you."

"That's right." Maddie's father spun the wheel as he turned onto the freeway. "Something like this could lead to big things. Maybe even a college scholarship."

Maddie shrugged. College was a long time away. Riding was now. And she didn't want to miss one minute of time with Cloudy—especially if there was a chance she might not be able to ride her much longer.

She hesitated as she thought about the Richardson Situation. Would she still be as excited about riding if Cloudy ended up leaving the barn?

But she shoved the thought away as quickly as it had come. Ms. Emerson had told her not to worry about it yet, and Maddie was trying really hard to obey.

The next day, bright and early, Maddie rode her bike to the barn. There were no regular lessons scheduled on Mondays, which made it the perfect time to visit Cloudy. Maddie often went to the barn just to give the pony a bath or take her out to hand graze or just hang out with her.

And today, spending time with Cloudy seemed more important than ever. The family trip to San Francisco had been fun, and distracting enough to make Maddie forget about the Richardson Situation—mostly, at least. But as soon as she was back at home, it seemed to be all she could think about.

She skidded around the corner into the stable's hard-packed drive, sending puffs of yellowish dust up all around her. Dropping her bike in the gravel yard outside the door, she hurried into the barn. It was nice and cool inside, thanks to the fans and the cross-breeze from the two big open doors at either end.

The only person in sight was the local farrier, a burly young man named Buzz. Maddie wasn't sure whether that was really his name or if people just called him that because of his blond buzz cut. Every time she asked, Buzz turned it into a joke, seeming to enjoy keeping her guessing.

At the moment the farrier had one of the lesson horses, a tall bay mare, in the crossties. One front hoof was propped on his leg as he trimmed it. When he heard Maddie coming, Buzz set the hoof down, then straightened up and stretched.

"Hi there, Madison Avenue." That was his favorite joke version of her name, though he had lots of others— Dolley Madison, Madison Wisconsin, Madison Square Garden. "How's it going?"

"Great." Maddie patted the horse. "Do you know where Ms. E is?"

"Not sure." Buzz mopped the sweat from his forehead with a rag. "Think she might've gone to turn out a couple of ponies."

"Oh." Maddie hadn't seen the barn owner in the small paddocks beside the barn. That meant she'd probably taken the ponies down to the slightly larger turnout field at the far end of the long, narrow property. If so, it could take her a while to return, and Maddie didn't want to wait. "Um, if you see her, could you let her know I'm taking Cloudy out for a walk?"

"Sure, no problem." Buzz flexed his hand, then bent to pick up the horse's hoof again.

Maddie thanked him and hurried off toward Cloudy's stall. She was sure her plan would be okay with Ms. Emerson. The barn owner liked it when students took their favorite mounts out to hand graze or just go for a walk. Most of the horses and ponies got about half a day's turnout on most days, but they always appreciated the chance to get outside and stretch their legs for a few extra minutes. When Maddie had mentioned this once to her Pony Post friends, Haley and Brooke had been surprised. Both their ponies lived outside, only coming into their stalls during bad weather. That was pretty normal where they lived—Haley on a farm in Wisconsin and Brooke in a rural part of Maryland's Eastern Shore. But Nina had understood. She lived in New Orleans, and city horses had even less turnout space than the ones in Maddie's overcrowded section of Northern California.

"I bet you'd love to be outside all the time, though, wouldn't you?" Maddie said as she clipped a lead rope to Cloudy's halter. "That's what you were used to when you were a baby back on Assateague Island."

Cloudy nickered and stepped toward the door, as if asking why Maddie was standing around talking when they could be heading outside. Maddie smiled and led her out of the stall.

They emerged out the far end of the barn. Grass was hard to come by in the summer, when it often didn't rain for months. But there were a few spots where there was enough for a little grazing, and the horses always seemed to appreciate even a few mouthfuls of the green stuff.

Maddie knew of a good spot by the paddocks on

the opposite side of the barn from the riding ring. Soon Cloudy was nibbling eagerly at the tufts of grass along the fence line.

For a few minutes, Maddie just stood and watched her. When the pony had exhausted the sparse supply of grass, Maddie pulled a peppermint out of her pocket.

"Okay, Cloudy," she said. "Do you want a treat?"

The pony's ears pricked forward, and she stretched her nose toward Maddie's hand. But Maddie stopped her.

"No, no," she said. "You know how to ask. One foot up! Up!"

She pointed at the pony's front leg and snapped her fingers. Cloudy snorted, lifting her hoof off the ground and then dropping it again.

"Good girl!" Maddie cried with a grin. She'd been working on this latest trick with Cloudy for the past few weeks. Vic sometimes teased her for treating Cloudy like a big dog, but Maddie didn't mind. She couldn't have any house pets because of Ryan's asthma, so Cloudy had to be dog, cat, and pony to her.

The thought made her smile waver. Cloudy made her

life so much more complete. How could it even be a possibility that she might lose her?

"You can't go anywhere," she whispered fiercely, wrapping her arms around the pony's warm, solid neck. "I need you."

The pony stood quietly for a moment, seeming to enjoy the hug. Then she lifted her head, staring at something over by the barn with ears pricked.

Maddie stepped back, breathless at how beautiful Cloudy looked when she was standing at attention like that. She could have been one of her wild ancestors, lifting her head from the sparse native grasses of Assateague Island to stare at a gull wheeling in the distance. . . .

"Maddie!"

Ms. Emerson's stern voice pulled Maddie out of her reverie. The instructor had just emerged from the barn, followed by Mrs. Richardson and an equally tall, lanky man with graying hair who Maddie guessed had to be Mr. Richardson. Cloudy had heard them coming before Maddie had.

Ms. Emerson hurried forward. "I've been looking all

over for Cloudy." Her voice was clipped and she sounded annoyed. "I was expecting to find her in her stall, where I left her."

"Sorry," Maddie said. "Didn't Buzz tell you I took her out?"

"Buzz isn't a messenger service." Ms. Emerson glanced at the Richardsons. "Sorry about that, but no worries. Let's get her inside so the girls can tack her up."

Ms. Emerson took Cloudy's lead rope and led her into the barn, with the Richardsons walking beside her. Maddie trailed along as they brought the pony to the crosstie area. Felicia Richardson was waiting there with an armful of brand-new-looking grooming tools. Her younger sister was with her, though Amber and their young brother were nowhere in sight.

"Yay, you found her!" Felicia's face lit up when she spotted Cloudy.

"Yes, Maddie just took her out to graze." Ms. Emerson sounded less annoyed now. "Would you like me to show you how to clean her feet, Felicia?"

"Filly!" Felicia said.

"She's too old to be called a filly," Maddie spoke up, trying to be helpful. "Cloudy is a mare."

Felicia giggled. "No, *I'm* Filly," she explained.

Mrs. Richardson sighed. "This is the latest thing," she told Maddie and Ms. Emerson. "Felicia has chosen a new nickname for herself."

"Right—call me Filly." She beamed at all of them, then grabbed a hoof-pick. "Okay, what do I do?"

Maddie watched as Ms. Emerson gave Filly a grooming lesson. The younger sister helped with some of it as well. Soon the mare was tacked up and ready to go.

"Can I lead her to the ring?" Filly asked eagerly.

"I'll do it this time," Ms. Emerson told her. "Maybe you can lead her back after your ride."

"Okay." Filly skipped ahead as the barn owner led Cloudy down the aisle.

The other Richardsons followed. Mrs. Richardson paused and smiled at Maddie. "Would you like to come watch?" she asked. "I'm sure Filly won't mind. She's not shy."

Her husband laughed. "That's for sure!"

"Um, sure, thanks." Maddie fell into step with them.

Filly's younger sister stared at her curiously, seeming to notice her for the first time. "I'm Baby," she said. "Who are you?"

"I'm Maddie. Wait, did you say your name's Baby?"

Mrs. Richardson chuckled. "Her real name is Barbara," she explained. "But she's the youngest of six, so the nickname just stuck."

So weird nicknames run in the family, Maddie thought, glancing ahead at Filly, though she didn't say it out loud.

Filly turned out to be an even less experienced rider than Amber, though she also seemed much more willing to listen and learn from Ms. Emerson. The lesson went pretty well—Filly caught on to posting without much trouble, and even stayed in two-point position through a set of trotting poles.

"I think that's enough for today," Ms. Emerson said after Filly's third time through the poles. "We'll let you try a canter next time, all right?"

Maddie expected Filly to protest, given her older sister's behavior. But Filly beamed, seeming delighted with the whole experience.

"That was fun!" she exclaimed. "Thanks, Ms. Emerson. And thanks to you too, Cloudy!" She leaned forward and gave the pony a big pat.

"Can I try?" Baby piped in from her spot on the fence near Maddie.

"Oh, Baby," Mrs. Richardson began. "I don't know if Ms. Emerson has time to—"

"It's all right." Ms. Emerson smiled at Filly. "You don't mind if your sister goes for a short pony ride, do you?"

"Nope." Filly kicked her feet out of the stirrups and slid down. She gave Cloudy a hug, then took off her helmet and handed it to her sister.

As Baby's father lifted his youngest daughter into the saddle, Filly wandered over to where Maddie was standing. "Did you have fun?" Maddie asked politely.

"Definitely!" Filly's face lit up. "Cloudy's the best. I can't wait until I can ride her every day. But I can already tell she and I have a special bond."

Maddie's heart sank as Filly started chattering eagerly about all her plans for Cloudy. Maddie had been trying to look on the bright side and not assume Cloudy was leaving, but what was the point in denying reality? There was no way anyone *wouldn't* fall in love with Cloudy—especially a horse-crazy girl like Filly.

So that's it, I guess, Maddie thought, feeling as if her heart might break. *The Snack and Swim will probably be my last ride on Cloudy. I might as well just try out for the Cascade League after all and forget about riding. . . .*

She watched as Cloudy stepped carefully around the ring, one ear pointed toward Ms. Emerson, who was leading her, and the other at the tiny girl bouncing happily on her back. But when they passed the spot where Maddie and Filly were standing, the pony flicked both ears toward them.

"Hi, Cloudy!" Filly sang out, seeming to think the pony was looking at her.

But Maddie knew better. Cloudy was looking at *her*. She was *her* pony at heart—they were meant to be together. *She* was the one who had the special bond with Cloudy.

And Maddie wasn't about to give that up. No way. She had to figure out a way to stop this sale from going though—no matter what.

◆ CHAPTER ◆

5

"MADDIE! I'M WIDE OPEN!" A KID NAMED Jack hollered, dancing back and forth on the spongy, well-irrigated grass of the high school soccer field.

Maddie dribbled the soccer ball between her feet, keeping an eye on the boy hovering to her right. But she forgot about the girl on her left. When she tried to pass the ball to Jack, the girl jumped forward and intercepted.

"Ha!" the girl cried as she quickly passed to one of the other kids on her side of the drill.

Coach Wu blew her whistle. "Sorry, guys," Maddie called to Jack and the others who were playing on her side. "Guess I flubbed that one."

"Just don't do it in a real game," a girl warned.

"Yeah, hotshot." Jack grinned, tossing his bright red hair out of his eyes. "You might not want to do it when the Cascade League scouts are watching either, or they'll take back that invite."

Maddie grinned as the rest of the team laughed. They'd been ribbing her since practice started. She didn't blame them. It was good-natured, and she'd have done the same if any of them had been chosen.

Coach Wu jogged over. She was in her late twenties, petite and kind of hyper, with a quick smile that showed her gums.

"Okay, people," she said. "Let's talk strategy here. . . ."

The coach spent the next few minutes discussing the drill they'd just finished, but Maddie's mind wandered after about thirty seconds. She'd spent the past twenty-four hours trying concoct a plan to stop the Richardsons from buying Cloudy, and she was pretty sure she'd finally come up with something that could work. Now she couldn't wait to get home and put it into action.

The rest of soccer practice seemed to drag on forever. But

finally Coach Wu released them. "Maddie, hold up a sec," she added as the rest of the team took off. "We should talk."

Swallowing a sigh, Maddie walked over to her. "What's up?"

"I found out more about the tryouts," the coach said. "They haven't nailed down a date yet, but they're working on it. I'm guessing you'll probably have at least a week to prepare, and then . . ."

Once again, Maddie couldn't seem to focus on what the coach was saying. She did her best to nod and smile at the right spots. What difference did it make? As soon as she was sure Cloudy wasn't going anywhere, Maddie would break the news to Coach Wu that she wasn't trying out for the travel team.

When she got home, Maddie hurried up to her room and logged on to the Internet. There were several new e-mails in her in-box, including one from her friend Bridget, who was away at performing arts camp for the entire summer. But Maddie barely skimmed Bridget's news about theater tryouts and cute band boys before clicking the e-mail shut, telling herself she'd read and respond to it later. Then she Googled Amber Richardson's name, and the first entry that popped up was the girl's Facebook page. Maddie quickly sent Amber a Friend request, along with a message:

> Hi Amber! It's Maddie, from Solano Stables.
> Remember me? I'm having a lesson on
> Cloudy tomorrow (Wed) @ 3 and I thought
> u might want to come and watch. That way
> u can see what Cloudy is really like.

She hesitated for a second, reading over the message. Then she scrolled down and added one more line at the bottom:

> Bring your sisters & your parents if u want, too.

She sent the message, not giving herself a chance to lose her nerve. Then she swallowed hard, fighting off a twinge of guilt. Was she doing the right thing?

Closing her eyes, Maddie pictured Cloudy standing there yesterday, head up, ears alert, mane blowing in the breeze. The little Chincoteague mare was so beautiful, so special in every way. How could Maddie just sit back and accept that she might never see her again? No, she had to do something to stop her from leaving.

"Whatever it takes," she murmured aloud.

She clicked back to her e-mail account. Below Bridget's e-mail were several more new messages. One was from another friend and a second was from Maddie's grandmother in Arizona, but the rest were notifying Maddie of recent entries on the Pony Post. Oops. Maddie realized she still hadn't checked in with her friends there. What with the trip to San Francisco, soccer practice, and of course her worries about Cloudy, she just hadn't quite gotten around to it.

"Better post something or Nina will call out the National Guard or something," she muttered, logging on to the site.

Sure enough, there were several concerned posts among the usual chitchat about ponies and such:

[NINA] Did I miss any posts from Maddie? B/c I haven't seen anything from her since she put up those pix

[HALEY] If u missed them, I did too. Hope she's OK!

[BROOKE] Me too. Should one of us try calling her?

[NINA] Nah. She's probably just having so much fun w/Cloudy that she forgot about lil old us. But she better remember soon! Maddie? Paging Maddie! Where are u?

[BROOKE] Or maybe u were right, Nina— maybe she met a movie star and ran off to Timbuktu!

[HALEY] Why would a movie star go to Timbuktu?

[BROOKE] lol lol why not? Movie stars can go wherever they want to!

[HALEY] Where is Timbuktu, anyway?

[NINA] Who cares where it is? Maddie wouldn't run off to Timbuktu, not even w/the coolest movie star ever. Not unless she could take Cloudy along!

[HALEY] They make special planes that can fly horses overseas. I saw a thing about it on TV.

[NINA] OK, whatev. I srsly doubt Mad and Cloudy are jetting off to Timbuktu, or Paris or London either. But I hope M checks in soon . . .

"I know, I know," Maddie muttered, clicking open a new text box.

First things first: she wanted to make sure her friends knew she was okay, and definitely *not* in Timbuktu. Her fingers flew over the keys, and seconds later her message posted:

[MADDIE] Hi guys! Sorry I haven't posted—busy weekend! Went to San Fran w/the fam, had my lesson, soccer, etc. But I'm here now! Gotta go

catch up on your posts—more in a sec.

Almost instantly, two new posts popped up after hers:

[BROOKE] Yay! She's back!

[HALEY] Hi Maddie! Sounds like u had a fun

weekend!

Maddie scrolled up, scanning the rest of the posts from that weekend. Haley had written about her daily rides on Wings, the spunky pinto gelding she leased from her neighbor. The two of them competed in the sport of eventing whenever Haley saved up enough money to pay entry fees. That wasn't very often, but Haley still took their training seriously.

Then there was Nina. She hadn't ridden on Sunday because she'd gone to an art gallery opening with her mom instead. But she and her pony Bay Breeze, better known as Breezy, had ridden with some friends on

Monday afternoon. Nina mostly did basic hunt seat riding in the ring at the stable where she boarded, but occasionally she got the urge to try something new, like setting up an obstacle course or trying her hand at saddleseat riding. Breezy sounded like a good sport about all of it, and Maddie could tell he was almost as special as Cloudy.

Brooke lived just a short drive from Chincoteague. She was the only one of the foursome who'd actually attended the world-famous pony penning and auction. That was where she'd bought her pony, Foxy, four years earlier. These days Brooke was busy teaching the young mare to jump, though the two of them spent most of their time trail riding or practicing their groundwork in the grass ring Brooke had created in her backyard.

Maddie always loved hearing about her friends' adventures with their ponies. But today reading the posts gave her a pang of envy. Her friends never had to worry about having their ponies taken away. Meanwhile it had always been in the back of Maddie's head that she could be separated from Cloudy if her mother was transferred to another Air Force base, though she'd tried not to think about that much. Now? She knew it might happen even sooner.

A new thought struck her as she scanned the others' posts. If she lost Cloudy, would she lose her connection to her Pony Post friends too? They'd all bonded over their Chincoteague ponies, but if Cloudy was sold, Maddie would be left with nothing but her battered old copy of *Misty of Chincoteague*. What if the others decided they didn't have anything in common with her anymore?

Maddie couldn't stand the thought. It didn't seem fair, especially since the Pony Post had been her idea in the first place.

She stared at the empty box for a moment, not sure what to say. Finally she started typing:

[MADDIE] Wow, sounds like u all did lots of fun stuff over the w/e! Me too—trip to SF was a blast, and I hung out w/Cloudy yesterday. We're all signed up for the Snack & Swim ride next Sun—can't wait! OK, gtg—just got home from soccer and I need a shower. Talk to u later!

She posted the message, then logged off. Maybe she'd tell them about the Richardson Situation later—*after* it wasn't a Situation anymore. Because she was more determined than ever to make her plan work tomorrow.

It *had* to.

• CHAPTER •
6

MADDIE FELT A FLUTTER OF NERVES AS SHE
coasted into the driveway of Solano Stables the next day.
Could she pull this off?

Dropping her bike in the usual spot, she checked her
watch. Almost an hour and a half before her lesson was
scheduled to start. That gave her an hour until the time
she'd asked Amber to meet her. The older girl had mes-
saged her back the day before, saying she'd be there.

"No turning back now," Maddie murmured as she
hurried into the barn.

She made a quick stop in the tack room to grab a
few grooming tools, then headed down the aisle toward

Cloudy's stall. The side door was open and Maddie paused to look out at the ring as she passed. Three little kids, maybe six or seven years old, were having their group lesson. At the moment, the girl on Wizard appeared to be trying unsuccessfully to convince him to step over a pole on the ground. Wizard kept stopping and dropping his nose to sniff at it, which caused his rider to break into uncontrollable giggles. The other two young riders were letting their ponies wander around on loose reins as Ms. Emerson focused on the first girl.

"It's a madhouse out there, isn't it?" a friendly voice commented.

Maddie glanced over and saw a woman standing in the shade of the overhang just outside the door. "Oh, hi, Mrs. Scott," she said. "I didn't see you there."

Maddie didn't know all the parents who brought the younger kids to lessons, but Mrs. Scott's husband worked at the Air Force base with Maddie's mother, and her older son played on one of the other teams in Maddie's league. She was an energetic, outgoing woman with a nose ring and a stylish short Afro. Her daughter was the rider who was still trying to convince Wizard to step over the pole.

"Jada looks good out there," Maddie added politely.

"No she doesn't." The woman laughed and glanced out at the ring as Wizard took a lazy step backward. "But she loves it, and that's what matters, right?"

"Definitely." Maddie smiled, preparing to move on.

But the woman stopped her with a hand on the arm. "By the way, congratulations, Maddie. Caleb told me you were selected to try out for the Cascade League. That's big news!"

"Oh." Maddie gulped. Somehow, she hadn't realized people knew about that already. Then again, why wouldn't they? Once Coach Wu had told the other Pelicans, it was only a matter of time before the whole league knew. Including Caleb Scott. And now his mother. And soon everyone in about a twenty-mile radius, given the way the local gossip mill worked . . .

"So when is your tryout?" Mrs. Scott asked eagerly. "You must be so excited!"

"Yeah." Maddie forced a smile. "I'm not sure yet when the tryouts start. Not for a week or two, I think."

Mrs. Scott nodded. "Good, good. That will give you

plenty of time to get nice and nervous, right?" She winked. "Just kidding. I know you'll do great, Maddie. We're all rooting for you."

Just then a cheer went up in the ring. Glancing over, Maddie saw that Jada Scott had finally gotten Wizard over the pole. The little girl was grinning proudly as her two friends whooped and pumped their fists.

"Good job, J!" Mrs. Scott called out.

"Um, see you later," Maddie said quickly, taking advantage of the woman's distraction to make her escape.

Soon she was in Cloudy's stall. The pony nudged her for a treat, but Maddie ignored her for a second, scanning the bedding. Good. There was a fresh pile of manure in the back corner.

When Cloudy nosed her again, Maddie fished a peppermint out of her pocket. "Okay, girl," she said, rubbing Cloudy's face as the pony crunched the treat. "Time to get ready. . . ."

She pulled a small comb out of her grooming bucket, then cast a slightly guilty look out at the aisle, hoping nobody passed by and noticed what she was doing. Because for once, she wasn't going to try to make Cloudy look better before her lesson. She wanted her to look worse. *Much* worse.

First the mane. It was long and silky and white, and normally Maddie loved combing it out so it lay flat and sleek against the pony's neck.

Not today. Grabbing a chunk of mane, she teased it with the comb until it was a snarled mess—creating what Ms. Emerson called a "witch's knot" because when ponies came in from the fields with them, it looked as if a naughty witch had tangled the hair during the night.

"Yuck," Maddie murmured as she wove a couple more knots into the mane.

She turned to Cloudy's tail next, creating another snarl halfway down. Next she dipped the end of the tail into Cloudy's water bucket, then sprinkled shavings over it. Some of the shavings stuck to the wet hair, and Maddie kneaded them in even further with her hands.

Cloudy's pale-gold-and-white-spotted coat looked pretty clean—but not for long. Maddie rubbed dirt and manure onto the pony, focusing particularly on her white legs and the big white spot that covered most of one side.

When she finished, Maddie stepped back and looked the pony over. "You're a mess!" she whispered.

She checked her watch. It was almost time for Amber to arrive. Grabbing the lead rope she'd left hanging over the stall door, Maddie clipped it to Cloudy's halter. She led her out and headed for the crosstie area.

On the way, she passed Vic and Val. The twins stopped short when they saw Cloudy.

"Whoa!" Vic exclaimed. "Did Cloudy find a mud puddle to roll in or something?"

Maddie shrugged. "Guess she's just a messy girl today." She hadn't told the twins about her plan, not wanting to jinx it. Besides, Val wasn't very good at keeping secrets— she tended to get nervous and blurt things out. "I'd better get started grooming her."

"Yeah, no kidding." Val shook her head. "Good luck. You'll need it."

"Thanks." Maddie continued on her way as the twins headed off in the opposite direction. She clipped Cloudy in the crossties, then walked all the way around her, wanting to get a better look in the bright light of the grooming area.

Just then she heard the chatter of voices from the end of the aisle. It was the Richardsons—Maddie recognized Filly's high-pitched, excited laugh right away.

"Okay, Cloudy," she whispered. "It's showtime!"

She grabbed a brush and ran it lightly over one of the dirty spots, being careful not to actually dislodge any of the carefully applied dirt. When the Richardsons' voices came closer, Maddie cleared her throat and started talking loudly to the pony.

"Oh, Cloudy," she exclaimed. "You're such a messy girl! One of these days my arms are going to fall off from having to do so much grooming before every single— Oh!" She pretended to interrupt herself as the Richardsons reached her. Amber was there, of course, along with Filly, Frank, and their mother. "Um, hi," Maddie added. "I didn't realize you guys were here already."

"Oh my." Mrs. Richardson gazed at Cloudy with mild alarm. "She's quite dirty today, isn't she?"

"Yes, but don't worry," Maddie said. "She's not usually

quite *this* dirty. Well, only about half the time. Anyway, it usually only takes me about an hour to clean her up before most of my lessons. Well, except during the rainy season, of course. . . ."

"That's weird," Amber said. "I don't remember her being that messy when we owned her before."

Maddie shrugged. "I guess ponies can change. Excuse me—there's a big gross stain on her other side that I should work on."

She hurried over to the pony's other side. Reaching into her pocket, she rustled the wrapper on a peppermint.

"Up," she whispered, hoping only the pony could hear. "Up, up!"

She snapped her fingers, keeping them hidden behind the pony's body. Then she held her breath, hoping Cloudy remembered how to do the trick.

The pony tipped one ear back as Maddie rustled the peppermint wrapper again. Then Cloudy lifted one foreleg, dangling it off the ground.

"What's she doing?" Filly wondered, pointing to the leg.

"I'm not sure," Maddie called to the younger girl over

the pony's broad back. "But you'd better stand back—just in case."

"What do you mean?" Mrs. Richardson sounded a little nervous as she pulled her son closer to her. "Is she going to kick?"

"She just gets a little excited sometimes, that's all," Maddie said. "Cloudy, no! Naughty! No pawing!"

"She never did that before either," Amber declared. "She must be getting tired of being a lesson pony. She'll probably be glad to get out of here and not have to do lessons anymore."

Maddie gulped. Uh-oh, she definitely hadn't been expecting *that* response. She peeked over Cloudy's back again. Mrs. Richardson had already let go of Frank. As Maddie watched, the woman pulled out her cell phone and started scrolling through it. The little boy headed off down the aisle toward a barn cat that had just wandered into view. Filly was sidling closer to Cloudy, not looking the least bit scared.

"Isn't your lesson starting in like twenty minutes?"

Amber spoke up. "Maybe we'd better help you get her cleaned up."

Maddie gritted her teeth as Amber grabbed a brush. "Okay, I guess," Maddie said. "Be careful, though."

"Whatever." Amber started scrubbing at a manure stain on the pony's rump. Filly stepped forward and set to work on the tangles in Cloudy's mane.

Maddie swallowed a sigh. Okay, so part one of her plan wasn't working quite the way she'd hoped. Good thing there was a part two.

Twenty minutes later, Maddie led Cloudy into the ring right on time. Vic and Val were already there with their ponies. They looked surprised when all four of the Richardsons filed into the bleachers.

"Aren't those the people who want to buy Cloudy?" Vic whispered, leaning closer to Maddie as their ponies touched noses. "What are they doing here?"

"Are they going to watch our lesson?" Val sounded nervous. She got self-conscious when her own mother stayed to watch her ride, let alone anyone else.

"Yeah, I guess so." Maddie busied herself with Cloudy's girth. Now that she was here, she wished she'd given the twins a heads-up. Maybe they could have helped with the plan. But it was too late to try to explain it to them now—especially since Ms. Emerson had just emerged from the barn.

"Everyone ready to ride?" she called out. Then she noticed the Richardsons. "Oh, hello! I didn't know you were coming today. I'm afraid Cloudy is already scheduled to be in this lesson."

"Oh, we know," Amber replied. "Maddie invited us to watch."

"She did?" Ms. Emerson glanced at Maddie with mild surprise. Or was that suspicion? Maddie wasn't sure.

The twins looked surprised too. But there was no time for questions. Ms. Emerson immediately started getting them on their ponies, and soon all three of them were walking around the outside of the ring.

Their usual warm-up consisted of walking the ponies around once each way, practicing leg yields and some basic bending exercises. Cloudy was good at all that stuff.

But today Maddie gave her an extra kick with her outside leg, the one Ms. Emerson couldn't see from the center of the ring. Cloudy lifted her head in surprise, but immediately veered toward the inside. When Maddie kicked again, the pony picked up a trot.

"Whoa, Cloudy!" Maddie cried loudly, leaning back in the saddle and pulling on the reins. "Easy, girl—don't get excited!"

"Maddie? What's going on?" Ms. Emerson asked.

"Nothing." Maddie steered Cloudy back onto the rail. "She's just raring to go, I guess."

"Hmm." The instructor raised an eyebrow. "All right, let's pick up a trot, please. Stay in your two-point halfway around the ring, then start rising. Remember to pay attention to your diagonals."

Maddie sent Cloudy into a trot again. But instead of releasing the pressure with her legs, she kept squeezing. Cloudy's ears flicked back, as if she was trying to figure out what Maddie was asking. After a moment she shook her head and broke into a slow canter.

"Whoa!" Maddie yelled again.

"Maddie," Ms. Emerson said sharply. "I asked you to trot."

"I know, but she's trying to run away with me!" Maddie exclaimed. She kicked with her outside leg again, causing Cloudy to speed up—and also veer in off the rail again. "Oh no, look out!" Maddie cried. "Aaah!"

She kicked her feet out of the stirrups and flung herself off the pony's side, landing on her rear end with an "oof!" and a puff of beige dust from the arena footing.

"Oh!" Val cried, pulling her own pony to a halt. "Maddie, are you okay?"

Ms. Emerson hurried over. "Maddie," she said. "What happened?"

"I—I'm not sure." Maddie tried to sound shaken and scared, even though she was neither. In fact, she wanted to grin at how perfectly her fake fall had gone—just the way she'd pictured it in her head! "She was out of control, and then I guess she bucked me off."

She made sure her voice was loud enough to carry to the Richardsons. Amber had already ducked into the ring and grabbed Cloudy by her flopping reins. The pony had stopped a few steps after Maddie had come off.

"Is she okay?" Amber called to Ms. Emerson. "Do you need me to get on and school Cloudy for you?"

Maddie gritted her teeth. Did Amber really think she could "school" Cloudy? Did she think she was a better rider than Maddie?

"Thank you, Amber, but that won't be necessary." Ms. Emerson sounded grim. "I think Maddie and Cloudy are finished for today."

"What?" Maddie blurted out. "No! I mean, I'm fine—I can get back on."

But Ms. Emerson was already marching over to retrieve Cloudy from Amber. She led the pony over and handed the reins to Maddie.

"Untack her and put her in her paddock," the instructor said in a voice only Maddie could hear. "And while you're at it, think about whether you really believe you should be allowed to go on the Snack and Swim ride after displaying this sort of childish behavior."

Maddie's face flamed. She might have fooled the Richardsons with her plan, and maybe even the twins.

But she should have known better than to try to fool Ms. Emerson.

"Sorry," she said, keeping her voice low so the others wouldn't hear. "I just—Um, sorry. But please, can I still go on the ride? I'll clean stalls every day for a month to make up for it!"

Ms. Emerson glanced over at the Richardsons. When she returned her gaze to Maddie, the barn owner's expression had softened slightly.

"All right, we'll need to talk about this incident later," she said. "I suppose since this is your first offense, the Snack and Swim is still on. But don't make me regret that."

"I won't—thanks. And sorry." Maddie was relieved, though her face was still flaming.

As she headed for the door, she sneaked another look at the Richardsons. Mrs. Richardson was bent over her cell phone as if nothing had happened. Amber was leaning back in her seat on the bleachers, looking bored. Filly was over by the fence, calling out questions to the twins about their ponies.

Maddie sighed. The Richardsons seemed totally

unfazed by Cloudy's "naughty" behavior. All that had happened was that Ms. Emerson had ended up annoyed at Maddie.

"So much for *that* plan," Maddie muttered as she led Cloudy into the barn.

A little over an hour later, Maddie was huddled with the twins in a shady corner of Cloudy's paddock. The mare was nibbling at a pile of hay nearby.

"I can't believe you tried to pretend Cloudy bucked you off." Vic giggled and glanced at the pony. "She never does anything like that!"

"I know, I know." Maddie had just finished filling the twins in on her plan. "It was a stupid idea. I just thought if the Richardsons saw her acting dangerously, they might not want to buy her anymore."

Val kicked at a stone, looking thoughtful. "I don't know," she said. "Cloudy was pretty bad when she got here. Your plan was worth a try."

"Thanks," Maddie said.

Vic was shaking her head. "Not really," she argued

with her twin. "I mean, yeah, Cloudy was bad when she got here. That's the point, right?"

"What do you mean?" Maddie asked.

"I mean, the Richardsons have seen her at her worst," Vic said. "They *owned* her at her worst. Nothing she does now is going to look all that bad to them, right?"

"I see what you mean." Maddie sighed. "I guess I didn't think about it that way."

"Never mind." Val reached over and gave Maddie's shoulders a quick squeeze. "We'll help you figure out a new plan."

"I don't know," Maddie said sadly. "If the Richardsons want to buy Cloudy and Ms. E wants to sell her, there's nothing I can do." Suddenly a thought struck her and her eyes widened. "Unless . . ."

◆ CHAPTER ◆
7

"UNLESS WHAT?" VIC DEMANDED. "DON'T keep us in suspense, Maddie!"

Maddie realized she'd gone silent, staring across the paddock at Cloudy as her brand-new plan filled her head and made her forget everything else. She turned and grinned at the twins, who were staring at her with wide, curious eyes.

"I just realized there *is* something I can do," Maddie told them. "I can buy Cloudy myself!"

The twins traded a look. "What?" Val said. "But the Richardsons already—"

"No, listen." Maddie was talking fast, working out the details as she explained them. "Ms. E would probably rather sell Cloudy to someone she knows will take good care of her, right? And who'd take better care of her than me?" She shrugged. "I mean, I'd want to board her right here at Solano Stables. So if I offer the same money or more than the Richardsons, Ms. E would probably be thrilled to sell her to me instead."

Vic gasped. "You know, that actually kind of makes sense!"

"Does it?" Val looked more skeptical than her twin. "Where are you going to come up with that kind of money, Maddie?"

"I don't know. I'm not even sure how much money we're talking about." Maddie drummed her fingers on the paddock fence. "I'll have to find out. In the meantime I can work on pulling together a down payment, and then figure out the rest from there."

"Maybe you could just ask your parents for the money," Vic suggested. "Maybe they'd buy you Cloudy as a late birthday gift or something."

Maddie's fingers froze. Oh, right—her parents. She'd been so busy formulating her new plan that she'd sort of forgotten about them. Including the part where she'd begged them to buy Cloudy for her past two birthdays and Christmases. And the answer had always been a firm no.

"I can't ask my parents," she told the twins. "They say we can't afford to own a pony."

"Oh." Val looked worried. "So what are they going to say if you buy her behind their backs?"

"Maddie can worry about that when it happens." Vic grinned. "Like I always say, sometimes it's better to ask forgiveness than to ask permission."

"Yeah," Maddie agreed. "And this is definitely one of those times."

She felt a bit troubled by the idea of going behind her parents' backs. Still, what choice did she have? This could be the only way to save Cloudy from going back to the Richardsons. Not to mention saving herself from losing the best pony ever.

Maddie was distracted as she wandered into her bedroom a little while later. Tillie was over by her dresser, applying lip gloss.

"Dad's running late at work," Tillie announced, smacking her lips together and then examining her face in the mirror from various angles. "But Nick's supposed to pick me up to go to the mall in like five minutes. Can you watch Ry and Ty until Dad gets home?"

"I guess." Maddie kicked off her paddock boots. "Where are they?"

"In the den, playing video games."

Maddie smirked. "In that case, they don't even need watching. They won't move until Dad gets home and takes a cattle prod to them."

Tillie grinned. "Later."

"Bye." As her sister hurried out, Maddie flopped onto her bed and reached for her laptop. The twins had helped her brainstorm ways to earn money, but they hadn't come up with many useful ideas so far.

Her fingers flew over the keyboard, going through the familiar steps to log on to the Pony Post. Nina was super-creative, Brooke was crazy smart, and Haley was one of the most practical people Maddie knew. If anyone could help her come up some great moneymaking ideas, it was the three of them. Of course, there was one problem—Maddie still hadn't told them about the Richardson Situation.

But mentioning that Cloudy might be sold—or even that Maddie wanted to buy her—would only bring a zillion questions, and Maddie didn't have time for that. Not when the Richardsons could make an official offer to buy Cloudy at any moment. She could fill her friends in later, once Cloudy was safely hers.

There were a few new posts from Nina and Brooke, but Maddie barely scanned them. She opened up a text box and typed fast.

[MADDIE] Hi all! Anyone have ideas for ways for me to make some $$?

[MADDIE] And don't say babysitting, lol. I need something that'll make me the big bucks fast.

After she sent the posts, Maddie sat back, staring at the screen without really seeing it. There had to be a way for her to make some quick cash. But what? She was pretty sure her parents wouldn't let her sell any internal organs. . . .

She blinked as her computer chirped. A new post had already popped up on the screen below hers.

[HALEY] Hi Maddie! Funny u should ask! My uncle just paid me to help him paint the barn. Not fun, lol, but I made enough to pay for another lesson w/my jumping coach.

Maddie glanced around her room, studying the walls. Painting a barn did sound hard, but maybe she could ask her parents if any of the rooms in their house needed repainting. That didn't sound too bad.

[MADDIE] Thanks, great idea! Well, not the barn part, lol. Any other brainstorms?

[HALEY] Maybe u could start a dog-walking business, or pet sitting? What do u need the money for, anyway?

Maddie's fingers hovered over the keys. What should she say? She didn't want to lie to one of her best friends. Maybe she could come up with something that was *sort of* true—just for now. . . .

[MADDIE] Remember how the Snack & Swim ride is coming up this Sunday? I'm hoping to buy something special for it. That's why I'm in a hurry.

[HALEY] Cool! You mean like new boots, or a new swimsuit or what?

"Mads? You in here?" Maddie's father poked his head into the room, still dressed in his scrubs.

Maddie sat up. "Oh! You're home." She felt a flash of guilt as she remembered she was supposed to be watching her younger brothers. Still, her dad was smiling, which meant Ry and Ty probably hadn't managed to kill each other or burn the kitchen down.

She quickly typed one last post:

[MADDIE] My dad just got home—gtg. Tx for the ideas!

She closed the computer. Her father stepped into the room.

"Did you hear the message from Coach Wu?" he asked.

"What message?"

"It's on the machine."

Maddie shrugged. "I didn't check when I got home from the barn."

"Oh. Well, she says the powers that be got their act together faster than expected, and the Cascade League tryouts are this Saturday afternoon." Her father grinned. "So you'd better start warming up your kicking foot!"

"Saturday afternoon?" Maddie had nearly forgotten about the travel team. "But I can't do it then—I have my riding lesson."

Her father's smile faded. "You can miss one lesson," he said. "Maybe you can ride on Sunday this week instead."

Maddie shook her head. "Sunday's the Snack and Swim." At her father's perplexed look, she added, "It's this big trail ride. I told you about it, and—never mind. Anyway, I don't want to miss my Saturday lesson, especially this week."

"Why? What's so important about this week?"

Maddie hesitated. The Pony Post girls weren't the only ones who were still in the dark about the Richardson Situation. Maddie hadn't told her parents about it either. "I just don't want to miss it," she said.

Her father didn't look impressed. "Listen, Maddie, I know you think riding is all you want to do these days. But don't be shortsighted. This soccer thing could be a big opportunity for you."

Maddie could tell he was getting annoyed. She was a little annoyed herself. Why couldn't her parents understand that riding was important to her?

But she bit her tongue, not wanting to start an argument right now. It would only distract her from what was really important.

"Okay, maybe you're right," she said. "I'll call Coach Wu back in a little while. But listen, have you noticed that the dining room is looking a little dingy lately?"

"The dining room?" He looked surprised by the sudden change of topic. "Not particularly. Why?"

"Well, it's just that I'd be willing to repaint it if you paid me," Maddie said. "Or any other rooms you want. What about the boys' room? Of course, I might have to charge hazard pay for even setting foot in there. . . ."

"Oh, I see." Her father sounded faintly amused. "Trying to earn a little spending cash, are you? Let me guess—seeing Tillie wave her new phone around is driving you crazy and now you want one of your very own?"

Maddie smiled weakly. "You know how it is. A girl needs her toys."

"Hmm. Well, the dining room walls look fine to me," her father said. "But if you're really willing to work for cash, I have another job for you. . . ."

An hour later, Maddie looked up as the door leading from the house to the garage banged open. Her brother Ryan peered out at her. He was holding a book with his finger stuck in it to save his page. His dark hair was tousled, and his glasses were slightly askew as usual.

"What are you doing?" he asked.

"What does it look like?" Maddie sat back on her heels, giving her wrist a break. She'd been scrubbing at a grease spot on the garage's cement floor for at least ten minutes, and it still looked as disgusting as ever.

Ryan shrugged. "Dad said he'll be back out to help in a little while. Oh, he also said to tell you not to forget to sort the nails and stuff on his workbench."

Maddie glanced at the tools, hardware, and random scraps of wood piled all over the large wooden counter built against the back wall. Ugh. It was going to take at least another hour in the hot garage to sort out that mess. Maddie swiped at the sweat beading on her forehead. Unfortunately, she forgot she was still holding the greasy rag.

"Oh, gross!" she exclaimed as she felt the sticky, gritty grease coat her skin.

Ryan let out a bark of laughter. "Whoa," he said. "You look like Batman!"

"Thanks a lot," Maddie muttered.

"Hey, Ty!" Ryan turned and shouted back into the house. "Check this out—Maddie's Batman!"

Maddie tossed the rag in his direction, though it only went a few inches before fluttering to the ground. "Get out of here, will you?" she said. "Either that, or get out here and help me."

"No thanks." Ryan grinned at her. "I have better things to do. Like stare at the wall."

He disappeared, slamming the door behind him. Maddie used the hem of her T-shirt to wipe the grease off her face. Why not? The shirt was already filthy.

She had better things to do too. Like just about anything that would get her out of this hot, dirty, smelly garage. They'd lived in this house for less than three years. How had the garage ended up crammed full of so much junk? For a second she was tempted to go into the air-conditioned house and tell her father that she'd quit.

But then she remembered why she was doing this in the first place. It was all for Cloudy. She pictured the mare the way she'd seen her earlier that day, happily eating hay in her paddock. At Solano Stables, where she belonged. Suddenly cleaning out the garage didn't seem so terrible after all. At least not compared to the possibility of losing Cloudy.

Keeping that thought firmly in mind, Maddie grabbed the rag from where she'd tossed it and set to work on the grease spot with renewed energy.

◆ CHAPTER ◆
8

"WILL YOU TURN OFF THE LIGHT, ALREADY?" Maddie grumbled, glaring at her sister.

"Chill. I'll be done in a sec." Tillie was standing in front of her mirror, running a brush over her chin-length wavy hair. Several bottles and tubes were arrayed in front of her, and as Maddie watched, Tillie set down the brush and picked up one of the bottles. She carefully squeezed a tiny dab of goo onto her finger and started rubbing it on her face in small circles.

Maddie was tempted to get up and switch off the overhead light herself. Let Tillie finish her stupid beauty routine in the dark!

But she was too exhausted to bother. Every part of her body ached. She hadn't been this tired in a long time—maybe ever.

After she'd finished cleaning the garage, Maddie had gone around to all the neighbors' houses looking for more work. And she'd found it. First Mrs. Bracken had hired her to clean all the windows in her entire house. It was only after the insides of the windows were all spotless that Maddie realized the woman expected her to do the outsides, too!

Then Mr. Janicek had practically begged Maddie to take his hyper boxer to the park and toss a tennis ball until the dog got tired. Easy money, Maddie figured. She liked dogs. But after an hour, she'd started to suspect that Bosco wasn't so much a dog as a perpetual motion robot programmed to chase that stupid tennis ball until the end of time. He seemed willing to go until he dropped, but Maddie wasn't. She'd given it another half hour and then taken him home. Luckily, Mr. Janicek had seemed thrilled, and even gave her an extra few dollars as a tip.

Next Ms. Levy had asked Maddie to weed the flower

bed in her front yard. That hadn't been so bad—at least Maddie got to sit down and rest while she worked. Although she'd realized that sitting on the ground might not have been the smartest idea when a colony of stinging ants decided to crawl up her shorts. Yikes! At least her brothers hadn't witnessed that one, or she would have been dealing with ants-in-her-pants jokes for the rest of her life.

Ms. Levy's next-door neighbor had noticed Maddie dancing around, shaking the ants out, and hurried over to make sure she was okay. When she heard that Maddie was looking for odd jobs, she'd hired her to prune her rose hedge. Which was about six feet high and covered in thorns.

By the end of the day, Maddie had been dirty and sweaty, covered with dog hair and scratches and itchy ant bites. Plus, her throwing arm—which also happened to be her scrubbing arm and her weeding arm—had felt as if it was ready to fall off.

Had all the work been worth it? Maddie wasn't sure. She'd ended up with a decent wad of cash, but she was pretty sure it wouldn't be enough for even a small down payment on Cloudy. And she'd just about run out of neighbors, at least until Mr. and Mrs. Himura got back from vacation. So what else could she do to earn some fast money? If she didn't make an offer on the pony soon, it could be too late!

"I need more ideas," she muttered.

"Huh?" Tillie glanced at her in the mirror. She was still busy rubbing lotion into her face.

"Nothing. Um, I just remembered I need to do something." Climbing out of bed, Maddie groaned as her leg muscles protested. Hobbling over to her desk, she sat down and opened her laptop.

As she logged on to the Pony Post, she checked the time. It was almost ten thirty, which meant it was even later in her friends' time zones. There was no way any of her friends would see her post tonight. But with any luck, they'd see it first thing in the morning and there would be more ideas waiting when she checked back tomorrow.

[MADDIE] Hi guys, it's me again! Still looking for moneymaking ideas. Please let me know if u can think of ANYTHING I can do to earn $$$ fast.

Has to be something I can do in the next 3 days.

Seriously, I'll consider anything, no matter how

crazy! Write back asap, pls! Thanks!

"Are you done?" Tillie asked as Maddie hit enter. "I want to turn off the light now."

She sounded slightly annoyed. Typical Tillie. Maddie had been waiting for like a million hours for her to finish her stupid beauty routines, and now Tillie was acting like Maddie was the one holding up bedtime. But it wasn't worth fighting about—not tonight.

"Yeah." Maddie closed her computer. "I'm done."

She crawled back into bed. Seconds later the room went dark, and a few minutes after that Tillie was snoring softly on her side of the room.

Despite her exhaustion, Maddie couldn't fall asleep. Her mind was racing, as fast and skittery as a wild pony dashing across the dunes of Assateague. What if she couldn't earn enough money fast enough to buy Cloudy? She couldn't stand the thought of losing her. The Richardsons had almost ruined her once—Maddie couldn't let that happen to Cloudy again.

She couldn't let it happen to herself, either. She loved everything about being at the barn and couldn't imagine giving it up. She'd miss the people too much—the twins and Ms. Emerson and Kiana and everyone else. She adored every single animal on the place, even Horace, the cranky old barn cat.

But she loved Cloudy best of all. How could she step into the barn knowing her special pony, her best friend, wasn't there anymore?

Then there was the Pony Post. What would happen if Maddie lost her only real connection to Chincoteague? She'd never had any trouble making new friends, and her family had moved around enough to give her plenty of practice. Plus, she'd never even met Nina, Haley, or Brooke in person. Even so, the thought of losing touch with them made her feel lonelier than she'd ever been, even on the first day in yet another new school. But how could they all help but lose touch if Maddie lost Cloudy? It wasn't as if Northern California was crawling with Chincoteague ponies. Besides, even another Chincoteague pony wouldn't be the same as her Cloudy. . . .

Blowing out a sigh, Maddie switched on the small lamp on the table beside her bed. Then she reached for her well-worn copy of *Misty of Chincoteague*, which she kept tucked into the bedside table's lower shelf. After a quick glance across the room to make sure her sister hadn't stirred, she opened the book, flipping forward to Chapter 3, her favorite part. Settling back against her pillow, she read the familiar words:

> Spring tides had come once more to Assateague Island. They were washing and salting the earth, coaxing new green spears to replace the old dried grasses.
>
> On a windy Saturday morning, half-past March, a boy and his sister were toiling up the White Hills of Assateague Beach. . . .

Maddie read on, trying to lose herself in the familiar adventures of Paul and Maureen Beebe and the ponies of

Chincoteague. But after barely half a chapter, she let the book fall into her lap. Reading it was usually a guaranteed way to put her in a good mood. But today it only reminded her of just how special Cloudy really was—and how terrible it would be to lose her.

Setting the book aside, Maddie switched off the light and closed her eyes. But it took her at least another half hour to finally fall asleep.

A shrill buzzing sound jerked Maddie awake. She sat up and rubbed her eyes. Bright sunlight was pouring in through the windows. How late had she slept? She glanced at Tillie's bed, which was neatly made.

The buzz came again, and Maddie realized it was her cell phone. She grabbed it from the bedside table and answered without bothering to check the readout.

"Hello?" she mumbled, her voice still fuzzy with sleep.

"Maddie? Is that you?"

Maddie rubbed her eyes with her free hand, trying to wake herself up. The voice sounded sort of familiar, but for a second she couldn't place it.

"Hello?" the voice said again. "It's me, Nina!"

"Nina?" Maddie sat bolt upright in her bed. No wonder she hadn't recognized the voice right away! She'd spoken to Nina and the other Pony Post girls on the phone before, but only a few times, and always with lots of advance planning. The last time had been a conference call that Nina's father had set up as a special treat for Nina's birthday back in March.

"Did I wake you up?" Nina sounded bright and alert. "I thought it was like nine thirty there. Did I mess up the time difference?"

"Um . . ." Maddie glanced at her alarm clock, which read 9:33. "No, you got it right. Don't worry, I'm up."

"Good," Nina said. "Because I need to talk to you, girl. We're all worried about you."

Maddie rubbed her eyes again, stifling a yawn. "Huh? Who?"

"Me and the girls," Nina replied. "Well, mostly Brooke to start. You know how that girl notices everything, right?"

"Sure, I guess."

"Well, she e-mailed me and Haley the other day to ask us if we thought you were acting weird. And once she mentioned it, I realized she was right—since when do you ever go like four days without a peep on the Pony Post?"

"Um . . ." Maddie wasn't sure what to say to that.

"Brooke was also the first one to see your latest post this morning." Nina laughed. "I guess that makes sense, right? She's a whole hour ahead of Haley and me. Anyway, she e-mailed us as soon as she saw it."

"Um, saw what?" Maddie asked, trying to focus her sleep-muddled mind enough to remember what she'd posted.

"Your desperate cry for help," Nina replied with a touch of drama. "It was, like, the last straw. Haley decided we needed to find out what was going on with you."

That sounded like Haley. She was a straightforward person—an action girl, as Nina had jokingly dubbed her once.

"So I volunteered to call you," Nina went on before Maddie could say anything. "I've got unlimited long distance on my cell phone, so it made sense for me to do it. So that's our story. What's yours? Spill it, Maddie—we're worried about you."

Suddenly Maddie couldn't hold back any longer. She

had to talk to someone who could understand what she was going through, and who better than one of her fellow Chincoteague pony lovers?

"It's Cloudy," she blurted out. "It all started on Saturday when I showed up for my lesson and found out I was on the list to ride a different pony. . . ."

The story spilled out of her in a torrent of words. Nina stayed pretty quiet through it all except for a few exclamations here and there. When Maddie finished, there was silence on the phone for a second.

"Wow," Nina said at last. "I can't believe this! I'm so sorry, Maddie—no wonder you were freaked out! I can't even imagine someone coming in and buying Breezy out from under me. It's horrible! Why didn't you tell us about this sooner?"

Maddie bit her lip, not sure Nina would understand the next part. She always seemed so confident, so carefree—the type of person who marched to her own beat and didn't worry about what other people thought of her. "Um, I guess I was worried about what you guys would think," Maddie said hesitantly.

"What do you mean? It's not like it's your fault those people want to buy Cloudy."

"No, not that." Maddie took a deep breath. "I just—I was afraid that if you knew I might not have a Chincoteague pony anymore, maybe I wouldn't be, you know, welcome on the Pony Post anymore either."

"What?" Nina's indignation was unmistakable even over the phone. "Are you crazy, girl? You really think we'd ditch you even if you *did* lose Cloudy? Not that that's going to happen," she added hastily. "We're going to help you fix this mess, *tout de suite*."

"Toot what?"

"*Tout de suite.*" Nina laughed. "That's just something our maid says all the time. It's French for 'right away.'"

Maddie felt a fresh spark of optimism. "So you'll help me come up with ways to make more money?"

"For sure!" Nina exclaimed. "That way nobody will ever be able to even *try* to take Cloudy away from you again. So what have you done so far?"

"Well, yesterday my dad paid me to clean out the garage, and then I went around to ask all the neighbors if they had anything they wanted me to do." Maddie gave her friend the short version of her long workday. "But I think I've done all the odd jobs my neighbors have right now. And Mom and Dad won't let me knock on the doors of people we don't know."

"I hear you." Nina sounded thoughtful. "Anyway, odd jobs will only take you so far. You need, like, a real business plan. Something that will net you some serious moolah."

Maddie smiled. Nina was always coming up with crazy words and phrases like *"tout de suite"* and "moolah" that most kids their age would never think to use. Maybe it was because her mother was an artist, or because she lived in New Orleans, which had always seemed a bit like a whole different country.

"Okay," Maddie said, leaning back against her pillow and switching the phone to her other ear. "Like what?"

"Didn't Haley post something about dog-walking?" Nina asked. "That could work, right? There's this guy my dad knows who totally supports himself by walking people's dogs all over the Garden District. He takes them out in shifts—six or eight dogs at a time, all day long. The dogs love him, and so do their owners. He's got a waiting list a mile long."

"That's cool. But remember, I need money fast," Maddie said. "It would take a ton of time to build that kind of business."

"True, true. But listen, that gives me another great idea. Why don't you talk to Ms. Emerson about setting up a payment plan?"

"A what?"

"A payment plan," Nina repeated. "You know—like when people buy cars and houses and stuff. They don't usually have all the money up front, so they borrow part of it from the bank or whoever."

Maddie wrinkled her nose in confusion. "Are you saying I should ask the bank to loan me money to buy Cloudy?" she said. "I don't think that will work—I'm just a kid, remember?"

Nina laughed. "No, no. I'm saying you should ask Ms. Emerson if you could make payments to buy Cloudy—say, a certain amount each month until the whole amount is paid off. If you come up with a real plan, with numbers and everything, it'll totally make you seem grown-up and serious about the whole deal."

"Do you think so?" Maddie hadn't really thought about it that way.

"Sure. It might even be exactly what she needs to decide to sell Cloudy to you instead of those other people." Nina sounded confident. "Besides, it means you don't have to wait any longer to tell her you want to buy her."

"That's true." Maddie chewed her lower lip, thinking it over. "I guess maybe it's worth a try, anyway."

"For sure," Nina agreed. "You don't want her to finalize a deal with the other people while you're out somewhere pulling weeds or whatever."

Before Maddie could respond, there was a knock on the door. Her father stuck his head in. He looked surprised to see her still in bed.

"Better shake a leg, lazybones," he said. "We're supposed to leave for your soccer practice in twenty minutes."

"Oh, right. I'll be down in a sec." When Maddie's father disappeared, she spoke into the phone again. "Sorry, Nina. I have to go get ready for soccer. But I'm really glad you called.

And I'm sorry I didn't tell you what was going on right away."

"You're forgiven—this time," Nina said with a laugh. "But don't let it happen again."

"I won't. Um, can you let Brooke and Haley know what's going on for me? And tell them I'm sorry too?"

"Sure. Post later and let us know how things are going, okay?"

"Definitely. Thanks, Nina." Maddie hung up the phone and jumped out of bed, already feeling much more optimistic about the whole situation. She also felt silly for not telling her friends what was going on until now. She should have known they'd want to help—and that they'd never turn their backs on her, no matter what.

Knowing that made her feel like she could do anything.

"Thanks for the ride, Dad." Maddie unsnapped her seat belt. She could see her teammates milling around on one of high school playing fields. The grass looked extra-bright against the sere browns of the summer-scorched hills beyond.

"Hang on a sec." Her father put the car in neutral. "Did you ever call the coach back about that tryout on Saturday?"

Maddie gulped. She'd been hoping he'd forgotten about that.

"Um, not yet," she said. "But I'll talk to her now."

Her father frowned. "Maddie, this Cascade League thing is a big deal," he said. "If you don't start taking it seriously . . ." He sighed, letting his voice trail off. Then he cut the engine.

"What are you doing?" Maddie asked as he opened his door.

"I'm going to talk to your coach," he said. "I want to make sure all the arrangements are set so I can take time off work if necessary."

"You don't have to do that." Maddie hopped out of the car, hurrying around to his side. "Seriously, Dad. I'll talk to her, I swear!"

"It's no trouble, Mads. I'm already here." Her father strode off toward Coach Wu, who'd just appeared at one end of the field.

Maddie grimaced, hoping her father wouldn't embarrass her too much in front of the team. In any case, it looked like she was stuck—she would be going to that tryout whether she liked it or not.

◆ CHAPTER ◆
9

AFTER SOCCER PRACTICE, MADDIE STOPPED at home just long enough to change clothes, then grabbed her bike and headed to the barn. When she arrived, the parking lot was full. Thursdays were always busy—there were two back-to-back group lessons, followed by several privates.

"Hi, Maddie!" a high-pitched voice called out as soon as Maddie entered the barn.

Maddie squinted, trying to force her eyes to adjust from the bright sunshine outside. A little girl with sleek black braids was waving at her from the doorway to the tack room, grinning from ear to ear.

"Hey, you!" Maddie called back brightly. "How's it going?"

She recognized the girl, though she couldn't remember her name. A couple of weeks earlier, Maddie had been passing by the grooming area on her way to see Cloudy. She'd noticed that the little girl was having trouble convincing Wizard to pick up his feet so she could clean them out with the hoof-pick. Maddie had stopped and showed her how to get the pony to pick up by gently squeezing his chestnuts, the calluses on the inside of his legs. Ever since, it was obvious that the girl was Maddie's biggest fan.

"I'm riding Peaches today in my lesson!" the girl announced now, sounding excited. "I never rode her before."

"You'll love her," Maddie assured her with a smile. "She's a sweetheart."

"Cool." The girl grinned. "Are you riding Cloudy today?"

"Not today." Maddie's smile faded slightly. "I just decided to stop by and visit her. I'd better go do that now. Have a good ride, okay?"

She hurried off toward Cloudy's stall. The mare heard her coming and stuck her head out, nickering softly.

Maddie let herself in and gave the pony a hug. "Hey, girl," she said softly. "I'm glad to see you, too. And don't worry." She leaned closer, whispering into Cloudy's fuzzy ear. "I have a plan. Soon we'll never have to worry about being separated again."

That reminded her of the real reason she'd come to the barn today. Giving Cloudy one last hug, she let herself out of the stall and hurried back up the aisle. She spotted Ms. Emerson helping a tiny kid lead the barn's smallest pony, Peanut, out of his stall.

As soon as the pony was safely cross-tied in the grooming area, Maddie approached the barn owner. "Oh, hi, Maddie." Ms. Emerson seemed a little frazzled. "I didn't know you were here."

"I just got here," Maddie said. "And I have to tell you something—I can't come to my lesson on Saturday. There's this special soccer tryout that day, and my dad's making me go."

"All right, thanks for letting me know," Ms. Emerson said. "Will you still be coming on the Snack and Swim on Sunday?"

"Definitely!" Maddie nodded vigorously. "I wouldn't miss that for the world."

"Good." Ms. Emerson turned away, pointing a finger at a girl who was tacking up a stout little bay gelding nearby. "Charlotte! Don't let your reins fall down by the horse's feet!"

Maddie took a step closer to the barn owner. "Listen, I wanted to talk to you about something else," she began.

"Can it wait?" Ms. Emerson glanced at her watch. "Every single kid showed up for today's beginner lesson, and Kiana's out sick today. . . ."

Maddie's heart sank. Ms. Emerson didn't seem to be in any mood to talk about payment plans. Still, the barn owner's words gave her another idea.

"Do you need some help?" she asked. "I mean, I've been trying to earn money doing odd jobs all week. I'd love to help out right here at the barn!"

Ms. Emerson gave her an appraising look. "Trying to earn some spending money, eh?" she said. "All right, you have a deal."

"Great!" Maddie grinned. Helping out at the barn definitely beat cleaning the garage! "What do you want me to do first? Should I go help the kids finish tacking up? That girl with the red hair looks like she's way behind the others."

"No, she needs to learn how to do that herself." Ms. Emerson stepped over to the supply closet nearby. Reaching inside, she pulled out a manure fork. "Here you go—I've been so busy, I haven't had a chance to pick stalls since this morning."

Maddie accepted the fork, staring at it in surprise. "You want me to clean stalls?"

The barn owner was already hurrying off down the aisle. "The wheelbarrow's right outside the back door, airing out," she called over her shoulder.

Maddie glanced toward the nearest open stall, which had several piles of manure in it. When making her offer to help out around the barn, she'd vaguely pictured herself assisting the younger kids as they groomed and saddled their ponies. Or maybe something like cleaning the lesson saddles and bridles, oiling them carefully and wiping down the bits.

But if cleaning stalls was what it took to get on Ms. Emerson's good side—and earn another few dollars toward Cloudy's purchase price at the same time—then that was what Maddie had to do. Clutching her pitchfork, she headed for the back door in search of the wheelbarrow.

"Ugh!" Maddie grunted as she threw all her weight against the handles of the wheelbarrow, tipping its contents into the muck pile. She'd lost track of how many loads of dirty shavings and manure she'd pulled out of the stalls over the past hour.

She blinked the sweat out of her eyes and headed back into the barn. Parking the wheelbarrow in the doorway of another unoccupied stall, she set to work.

A few minutes later, she heard the clatter of hooves and the chatter of excited voices. The group lesson had just ended.

Maddie glanced out to see if the pony whose stall she was cleaning was heading her way. Instead, she saw Ms. Emerson coming toward her.

"How's it going, Maddie?" the barn owner asked.

"Fine, I guess." Maddie rested her weight on her pitchfork. "Although I'm a little worried about sweating to death." She forced a smile to show she was joking, even though she really wasn't.

"It's pretty hot today, isn't it?" Ms. Emerson sounded sympathetic. "Tell you what. Maybe you need a change of scenery—and a little fresh air."

Maddie perked up. "Sure! What do you want me to do?" Visions of exercising school horses or leading ponies to the far turnout started dancing through her mind.

"The paddocks are a mess," the barn owner replied. "Make sure you pick up as much manure as you can—even the small chunks—so the flies don't get bad."

After half an hour in the midday heat scraping sun-dried manure off the ground, Maddie was just about ready to call it quits. Her arms had started aching again, and she had manure under her fingernails and dust on her clothes.

"There—spotless," she muttered as she tossed one last pile of desiccated manure onto her wheelbarrow. She glanced over the two adjoining paddocks she'd just cleaned, then at the others still waiting. Surely Ms. Emerson didn't expect her to do *all* of them, did she?

After she dumped the wheelbarrow, Maddie left it and the fork by the back door and headed inside. The last of the lesson kids had long since departed, leaving the barn quiet. The shade felt good after the relentless glare of the sun outside, and Maddie paused to enjoy the slight breeze from a nearby stall fan.

Then she heard noises down by the grooming area. When she glanced that way, her eyes widened. Amber Richardson was leading a fully tacked-up Cloudy toward the side door!

The older girl didn't seem to notice Maddie as she disappeared outside. Maddie was so focused on catching up to her that she almost crashed into Filly Richardson as she stepped out of the grooming area.

"Oh, hi!" Filly said brightly. She was leading another tacked-up pony, a cute little buckskin with a crooked blaze and long eyelashes.

"What are you doing with Doodle?" Maddie blurted out.

"I'm taking a lesson on him." Filly was all smiles as she glanced at the pony. "Amber wanted to ride Cloudy today, so Ms. Emerson said I can ride Doodlebug." She giggled. "Isn't that the cutest name?"

"Definitely." Maddie stared from Filly to the adorable buckskin pony and back again, her mind clicking into overdrive. Doodlebug was for sale—he belonged to a family whose kids had all outgrown him. The owners were allowing Ms. Emerson to use the sweet, placid, reliable pony for lessons until the right buyer came along.

Maybe Filly thought she was just riding Doodle in a lesson. But what if Maddie could convince her—and the rest of the family—that he was a much better match for them than Cloudy? Maybe they'd buy Doodle instead!

"Doodle's amazing," Maddie told Filly with a big smile. "You'll love him. He's probably the sweetest pony I ever met."

"I know. He's great." Filly stroked the pony's velvety nose. "I love him already."

"I'm not surprised." Maddie glanced toward the door. "Hey, do you mind if I watch your lesson? I always like seeing Doodle go. He's so adorable!"

"Sure, I don't mind," Filly said.

"Great." Maddie fell into step beside the younger girl, trying not to let on how excited and nervous she felt. This could be the perfect solution to the Richardson Situation! Maddie wouldn't have to come up with enough money to buy Cloudy herself—or figure out how to explain the whole deal to her parents. Cloudy could stay right where she belonged, at Solano Stables, and everything could go back to normal.

When they reached the arena, Mrs. Richardson and Filly's younger brother were already in the bleachers. Mrs. Richardson was bent over her phone, while Frank was poking at the dry dirt by his feet with a stick.

Ms. Emerson was in the ring, helping Amber adjust her stirrups. The barn owner raised an eyebrow in surprise when she saw Maddie walking with Filly. "Finished with those paddocks already, Madison?" she asked.

"Just taking a break." Maddie smiled her most innocent and hardworking smile. "I'll finish up after I catch my breath."

Ms. Emerson didn't respond, turning instead toward Filly. "Need any help checking your girth?"

Soon the sisters were mounted and walking around the ring on their ponies. Maddie leaned against the fence and watched as the lesson began. Amber was already doing better with Cloudy. Mrs. Emerson had to remind her to loosen up her reins a couple of times, but Cloudy didn't look nearly as annoyed as she had on Amber's first ride.

Then there was Filly. It was obvious she'd paid close attention at her first lesson. Her heels were down, her back was straight, and her hands were steady on the reins. More important, she seemed just as delighted to be riding Doodle as she had been on Cloudy.

"Looking good, Filly," Maddie called encouragingly as the little buckskin trotted past her on the rail. "You and Doodle look like you're really getting along."

"Thanks!" Filly turned and grinned at her.

"Eyes forward, Filly," Ms. Emerson called from the center of the ring as Doodle veered off track, moving so close to the rail that one of Filly's boots almost hit the next post. "Your pony tends to go where your eyes do, remember?"

"Sorry!" Filly called out, straightening the pony. "Is this better?"

The lesson continued. Ms. Emerson had the sisters practice steering around a course of cones, and when

Doodle almost stepped on one of them, Maddie couldn't resist calling out to Filly again: "More inside leg! Good job."

This time she noticed Ms. Emerson giving her the evil eye. Oops. She backed away, leaning against the barn wall in the shade to watch the rest of the lesson.

At the end, Amber begged again to try jumping Cloudy, and this time Ms. Emerson relented. She had the older girl trot up to a crossrail, which the mare cleared with minimal effort.

"May I try?" Filly called out.

"I suppose that would be all right," Ms. Emerson said. "Doodle is a very steady jumper. Just trot him up to the jump, then get in two-point position and grab a handful of mane."

"Okay." Filly looked excited as she turned the pony toward the crossrail. "Trot, Doodle!"

The steady little buckskin trotted to the jump and hopped over. Filly laughed out loud when she landed.

"That was fun!" she cried. "Can we do it again?"

Ms. Emerson smiled. "Maybe next time. I think the

ponies have worked hard enough for today. Let's take them inside and sponge them off, all right?"

Maddie stepped forward as the two girls led their mounts out of the ring. "I can help untack and bathe the ponies if you want," she offered.

Mrs. Richardson joined the group just in time to hear her. "How nice, Maddie," she said with a smile. "I'm sure the girls appreciate that. Don't you, girls?"

"Uh-huh!" Filly said brightly, while Amber just shrugged.

"So how'd you like Doodle?" Maddie asked the younger sister. "He's pretty great, huh?"

"Yeah. Did you see me jump?" Filly beamed. "That was so cool!"

"Doodle's an amazing jumper, and he's perfect for you to learn on." Maddie glanced at Cloudy. "Some ponies, like Cloudy, can be a little too springy. But Doodle is super-smooth!"

Amber shrugged again. "I didn't think Cloudy was that springy. Anyway, Raina and Tommy used to jump her all the time, and they did fine."

"Hmm." Maddie turned back to Filly as they all entered the shade of the overhang by the door. "Anyway, like I was saying, Doodle is a super teacher. If you keep riding him in your lessons, you'll probably be ready to start entering shows pretty soon."

"Really?" Filly's eyes lit up with interest. "That would be fun."

Maddie glanced toward Mrs. Richardson, but the woman wasn't paying attention anymore. She'd stopped outside to chat with Ms. Emerson. Oh well. Maddie was pretty sure that all she had to do was win Filly over to her side and the enthusiastic younger girl would do the rest. She followed the sisters as they led their ponies to the grooming area.

"So did Ms. Emerson tell you Doodle's for sale?" Maddie tried to keep her tone casual. "His owner is looking for the perfect new home for him. If you're interested, you could ask her about trying him again."

"Why would we be interested in that?" Amber's voice went sharp and wary. "We already have Cloudy." She shrugged. "Or at least we *will* have her again, pretty soon."

"I know. I'm just saying that Doodle—" Maddie began.

Amber didn't let her finish. "Forget it," she said flatly. "Cloudy is the only pony for our family. I mean, we're the ones who picked her out at the pony auction and brought her to California."

Maddie was pretty sure Amber had been too young back then to do much of the choosing at that auction, but she didn't say so. Besides, the older girl had already turned to her sister.

"I learned to ride on Cloudy, and so did Raina and Tommy, and so will you," she said fiercely. "She's better than any other pony."

"Okay." Filly sounded meek. "I was just saying I like Doodle, too."

Amber shrugged and glanced at Maddie. "Look, I know you've been riding Cloudy a lot, and you probably don't want us to buy her back," she said. "But don't worry, we'll probably still board her here. Maybe we'll even let you ride her if we're ever out of town or something."

Maddie could tell that Amber was trying to be nice. For a moment she tried to take comfort in what the older girl was saying. It was better than nothing, right? She'd still be able to see Cloudy, pet her and hug her and give her treats. Maybe even ride her occasionally, though she wasn't going to hold her breath for that part.

Suddenly a shout rang out from somewhere down the aisle. "What was that?" Amber looked up from unbuckling the noseband on Cloudy's bridle.

Maddie was ready for an excuse to get away from the Richardson girls. "I'd better go see," she said, hurrying off.

She found one of the adult boarders glaring at young Frank Richardson. The woman was holding a bridle and shaking it in his general direction. Based on the scolding she was giving the boy, Maddie quickly figured out what had happened. Apparently, Frank had found the boarder's expensive new bridle hanging by her horse's stall and had used it to try to lasso the cranky barn cat.

Mrs. Richardson and Ms. Emerson soon arrived on the scene as well, drawn by the yelling. Maddie sidled away, not really wanting to get involved. Besides, the incident only reminded her of the stories she'd heard about all the barns the Richardsons had been kicked out of before Cloudy came to Solano Stables. Even if the family decided to keep the mare there, who knew how long it would last?

That made her realize she couldn't give up. No way. She had to find a way to buy Cloudy herself. No matter what her parents said about it afterward.

· CHAPTER ·
10

[BROOKE] Happy Friday, Maddie! Just checking in to see how Operation Buy Cloudy is going! I hope u have a great day today—let us know how it goes!

[HALEY] Same here, Mad! I know you can do it—go go go! Get that pony! We're all thinking of you!

[NINA] Yeah, what they said! lol. Srsly, Maddie, you're like the most determined person I know. If anyone can make this work, it's def. u! Luv ya!

Maddie smiled as she read over her friends' messages a second time. Talk about a great way to wake up!

And she needed a lift that morning. She hadn't slept well—she kept waking up from weird dreams where Cloudy was trotting away from her and jumping into the surf crashing against the rocks near the Golden Gate Bridge. Maddie kept trying to stop her, knowing it was way too far for a pony to swim from there all the way around the globe back to Assateague. . . .

"Weird," she muttered, doing her best to banish the dreams from her thoughts. She didn't have time to worry about stupid stuff like that right now. Not when she still needed to figure out how to save Cloudy from the Richardsons.

She hadn't quite dared talk to Ms. Emerson the day before about buying the mare—not after the incident with Frank Richardson and the fancy bridle. No, Maddie wanted to make sure the barn owner was in the best possible mood when she brought up the subject. With any luck, she could make some more money today—maybe enough for a real down payment. Then she could talk to Ms. Emerson after the Snack & Swim ride, when all of them would be in a great mood.

Glancing again at her friends' cheerful, encouraging words on the computer screen, Maddie actually started to believe this could all work out. She hoped so, anyway. At least now she knew if she *did* lose Cloudy, she still had them. . . .

"No," she muttered under her breath. She couldn't think like that—she couldn't give up! Cloudy was too important. Maddie had to make it work out, no matter what!

Logging off the Pony Post site, she headed for the door. She didn't have soccer practice or riding lessons today. That meant she could spend the entire day out earning money for that down payment.

By dinnertime, Maddie was feeling discouraged. She'd made the rounds of the neighborhood once more, but just as she'd expected, not as many people had wanted to hire her this time. The Himuras had just returned from their trip and paid her a few dollars to weed and water their lawn, and Mr. Janicek had asked her to take Bosco to the park again. Other than that? Nothing. If things didn't pick up, it was going to take Maddie forever to earn enough money to buy Cloudy!

She picked at her food, barely hearing her sister's chatter about her super-important social plans for the weekend or Ry and Ty's arguments over who got the bigger pork chop.

"So, Mads," her father said, reaching for the salt. "Psyched for the big tryout tomorrow?"

"I guess." Maddie tried to sound more enthusiastic than she felt. "Don't get your hopes up, though, okay? Coach Wu says hardly anyone makes the cut their first time out."

Her father reached over and tugged on her hair. "Hardly anyone is as talented as my daughter."

Maddie's mother rolled her eyes. "Way to put pressure on the poor girl!"

But Maddie could tell her mother was joking. For some reason, she seemed just as excited as Maddie's dad about this whole Cascade League thing.

"Get real, Dad," Tyler said. "It'll be a miracle if Maddie makes it past the first cut."

Ryan looked up from his plate with a grin. "You know what's a miracle? That Mom and Dad actually convinced her to skip her prancy pony lesson to go to the tryout tomorrow."

Tyler snorted with laughter. "Yeah, that's a miracle all right—I thought they'd have to tie her up and throw her in the trunk of the car to get her away from the ponies! Prancy, prancy, prancy . . ."

"Whatever." Tillie speared a lima bean with her fork. "We all knew the horse thing wasn't going to last forever, right? I mean, this is Maddie we're talking about."

Maddie frowned as the rest of the family laughed. "Shut up," she told her sister. "I'm not the one who gave up all her other interests to start chasing boys like a pathetic loser."

"Maddie, that's enough!" her mother said sharply. "We're talking about you right now, not your sister. And you have to admit, you do have a history of being super-gung-ho about things and then giving them up cold turkey."

"Not this again," Maddie muttered. Would they ever get over the judo thing? "Riding's different."

"Okay." Tillie sounded skeptical. "Anyway, enough about that. Can someone drive me to the mall tomorrow morning?"

As the conversation wandered away from her, Maddie stared at her plate without really seeing it. Normally, her brothers' stupid jokes and insults didn't bother her. But for some reason she couldn't get Ryan's comment out of her head. Could he possibly be right? *Had* she given in too easily when her parents had insisted she skip her lesson to go to that tryout? She didn't usually defy her parents, but she could be stubborn when she felt strongly enough about something. When they'd packed up to move here from their previous home in Colorado, she'd locked herself in her room for almost an entire day until her parents had promised not to give away her beloved Flexible Flyer just because they were moving to a place where it never snowed.

But this time, she'd given up her lesson with barely a whimper. Did that mean she didn't feel as strongly about riding as she thought she did? Maybe it really was all about Cloudy. And now that she feared Cloudy might not be around much longer, maybe she was already starting to pull away. . . .

The thought made her feel anxious and uncertain, and she definitely didn't like feeling that way. Trying to shake it off, Maddie vowed to talk to Ms. Emerson as soon as possible. She'd just tell her the truth—she wanted to buy Cloudy, but she'd need some time to come up with the full amount. Maybe Nina could give her some tips on coming up with a payment plan. Or better yet, she could ask all her Pony Post friends for help—she knew Brooke had saved up to buy both her saddles, and Haley was always budgeting her allowance carefully to pay for her eventing lessons and competitions.

Having a plan made her feel better. With any luck, she'd be able to present her ideas to Ms. Emerson right after the Snack & Swim.

"By the way . . ." She spoke up suddenly, interrupting whatever Tillie was saying about her planned shopping spree. "Don't forget, I'll be gone all day Sunday at the Snack and Swim ride."

"The what?" Tillie wrinkled her nose.

"The Snack and Swim. It's a trail ride where we take our ponies swimming." Maddie felt a shiver of excitement as she thought about it. Lose interest in riding? No way, not her! "It's going to be a blast," she added. "I can't wait!"

"Awesome job, Maddie!" Coach Wu lifted her hand for a high five as Maddie jogged off the field. "You're on fire out there!"

"Thanks," Maddie said breathlessly.

The Cascade League tryout was taking place on the playing fields at the local community college. Maddie couldn't believe how many other kids were there. Some she recognized from the other teams in her league, while others were total strangers. But all of them were good— really good.

So am I, she reminded herself as she chugged from the water bottle Coach Wu handed her.

For a second her mind wandered forward in time to what would happen if she made the league. Could she really give up riding for the entire summer?

But no—she wasn't going to think about that right

now. She was just going to do her best at this tryout and worry about everything else later.

A whistle blew, and Coach Wu gave her a shove. "Get back out there and make me proud, girl," she said with a grin.

Maddie nodded, wiped the water off her mouth, and ran back out to take her position. She found herself facing off against a ridiculously tall, willowy girl with short blond hair. Everyone had been whispering about her all day—she was from some little town off to the east of Sacramento, and nobody could believe she was really only twelve, but everyone said she was the best dribbler in California. Supposedly, nobody in her home league could keep up with her.

Well, I'm going to show her she's not in her home league anymore, Maddie thought, clenching her fists and focusing everything she had on the scrimmage.

She might not be able to stop the Richardsons from wanting to buy Cloudy, or force her neighbors to hire her for odd jobs, or even convince her parents not to make her come to this tryout. But this? This was something she could do. She could show that tall girl that Maddie Martinez was a force to be reckoned with on the soccer field! The Richardsons, Ms. Emerson—even Cloudy—faded out of her mind as the whistle blew to start play.

By the time the tryout scrimmage ended, Maddie had intercepted the tall girl three times, stolen the ball from her once, and scored two goals. She was panting, her muscles were screaming, and she was dripping sweat from every pore, but she felt good. That had been fun!

Coach Wu was grinning as Maddie jogged toward her. "You know I'm a pessimist, right?" she said. "Even so, I'm thinking you have a good shot of making the league. You were awesome today, Maddie!"

Maddie smiled, but her mind was already wandering. "Thanks," she said, grabbing a bottle of water and chugging half of it.

"We should hear some results by the end of next week," the coach continued, tossing Maddie a towel. "Stay tuned, okay?"

"Yeah." But Maddie wasn't really thinking about soccer anymore. Her mind had wandered all the way back to Solano Stables. What was going on there today? Had Amber or Filly come to ride Cloudy? What if the

Richardsons made an offer to buy her before Maddie got a chance to talk to Ms. Emerson about her own proposal?

As soon as she got home, Maddie shut herself in her room and locked the door. Tillie was still at the mall, so she wouldn't come pounding on the door anytime soon, but Maddie didn't want any interruptions from her dad or the boys.

Not bothering to change out of her sweaty soccer clothes, she flopped onto her bed and hit one of the presets on her phone. Vic answered on the third ring.

"Hey, Maddie!" Her voice sounded cheerful, which gave Maddie hope that she hadn't missed anything too dramatic—like the Richardsons loading up Cloudy and taking her away to some other barn. "What's up? How'd your tryout go?"

"Fine," Maddie replied. "How were things at the barn?"

"Hold on a sec." Maddie could hear Vic talking to someone in the background—probably her twin. "It's Maddie."

A second later, Val's voice came on the line. "Hi, Maddie. We missed you in our lesson today."

"I missed you guys too." Maddie pressed the phone

tighter against her ear. "But listen, what else went on? Did the Richardsons ride Cloudy today?"

"They were supposed to," Val said. "Ms. Emerson was in a big hurry at first because Amber and Filly were scheduled to come ride Cloudy and Doodle right after our lesson. But they called while we were tacking up and canceled."

"Really?" Maddie said. "Why'd they cancel?"

"I don't know."

There was the sound of a scuffle and a peeved "hey!" from Val, and then Vic's voice came back on the line.

"Yeah, Ms. E was totally cheesed off. You could tell," she said. "I mean, they called just as we were getting ready to go out to the ring—that's only like an hour before they were supposed to be there!"

Maddie felt a flicker of hope. Ms. Emerson didn't have much patience for tardiness or no-shows or flakiness of any kind. Maybe she'd get fed up enough with the Richardsons to tell them to take a hike!

Then again, maybe she'd decide it was easier to stop giving them lessons and just sell Cloudy to them and tell them to take her to another barn. . . .

"So they didn't say why they weren't coming?" Maddie asked, trying not to dwell on that second possibility.

She could almost hear Vic shrug through the phone. "If they did, Ms. E didn't tell us," Vic replied. "So anyway, Cloudy got the day off. She should be nice and rested for the Snack and Swim ride tomorrow."

"Yeah." Suddenly Maddie had another thought. "Wait, did Ms. E tell the Richardsons about the Snack and Swim? What if they show up tomorrow expecting to have their lesson then?"

"Tough luck if they do," Vic replied. "She's not theirs yet, right? And you're already signed up to ride her tomorrow."

"Right." Maddie felt a little better. Ms. Emerson wouldn't pull the pony out from under Maddie after promising she could ride her on the Snack & Swim. Cloudy would definitely be all hers tomorrow.

Maddie just hoped it wouldn't be their last ride together.

✦ CHAPTER ✦

11

SUNDAY MORNING DAWNED BRIGHT AND sunny and not too hot—a perfect summer day. Maddie woke up before the alarm went off, feeling excited even before she remembered why.

Then she glanced at her swimsuit, which was hanging over the back of a chair near the bed, and remembered. It was the day of the Snack & Swim ride!

Hopping out of bed, she shut off the alarm and glanced across the room. Tillie even looked tidy and perfect when she slept—she was on her back, her dark hair perfectly arrayed on her pillow like a halo. Her pink silk eye mask covered half her face, and her sheet lay flat and straight over her body.

On another day, Maddie might have been tempted to mess with that perfection somehow—maybe put goofy eyeball stickers on the mask or hide a fake spider under the sheet. But she didn't have time for that sort of thing today.

Grabbing the clothes she'd set out on her chair the night before, she headed across the hall to the bathroom. After a quick shower, she pulled on her swimsuit and then her riding clothes. She gathered her hair into a ponytail without bothering to dry it—after all, it would only get wet again later.

Tiptoeing back into her room, she grabbed her laptop. Tucking it under her arm, she headed down to the kitchen.

"Morning, Mads," her father greeted her as the two of them passed on the stairs. "I'm going to jump in the shower; then I can drive you to the barn. Make sure you eat something before we go."

"Okay, thanks." Maddie continued into the kitchen. It was deserted, though she could tell by the coffee cup in the sink that her mother had already been there and left.

Maddie poured herself a bowl of cereal, then logged on to her laptop as she ate. When she loaded the Pony Post there were several new messages waiting for her.

[NINA] Good morning Maddie! Post something when u see this, because SURPRISE!—we're all here waiting to wish you well today!

[BROOKE] Right! For the Snack & Swim, and also your chat w/Ms. E.

[HALEY] I'm here too! Hope you check in before you leave for the barn or we're all going to feel rly stupid, lol!

[NINA] She'd better check in, or she's in big trouble! Ha ha!

"Aw, you guys!" Maddie murmured, touched that her friends had gone to the trouble of figuring out when she'd be likely to check in and making sure they were all online.

How could she ever have doubted their love and loyalty? She quickly opened a new text box.

[MADDIE] I'm here, I'm here! U guys are the best! But don't u have anything better to do on a Sunday morning than sit around waiting for me, lol?

She sent the post, then sat back and waited. It only took a moment for the responses to start coming.

[BROOKE] What could be more important than u?

[HALEY] Yeah. Besides, my uncle made pancakes & venison sausage for breakfast, and I'm too stuffed to move, lol!

[NINA] OK, enuf about what u all had for b'fast! I want to hear what Maddie decided about talking to Ms. E.

[MADDIE] To be honest, I haven't decided yet. When do u all think I should talk to her?

[BROOKE] I think you should just enjoy the S&S ride, then talk to her afterward.

[HALEY] I dunno . . . I'm not sure u should talk to her until you've saved up more $$$. Otherwise, she might not take u seriously, u know?

[BROOKE] But what if the R's make an offer in the meantime? My stepdad would say "The early bird makes the sale."

[HALEY] LOL! What does that even mean?

[BROOKE] I dunno, but he says it a lot, lol!

[NINA] Whatev, if it were me, I wouldn't be able to wait. I'd probably talk to Ms. E as soon as I saw her and get it out of the way so I could relax and enjoy the ride. That's just me—but I think Mad might be the same way, maybe???

Maddie bit her lip. Was Nina right? If she didn't talk to Ms. Emerson right away, would worrying about it ruin the ride?

Then again, the other two had good points as well. All along, Maddie had figured it might be better to wait until after the Snack & Swim, when Ms. Emerson would probably be much more relaxed. Or maybe Haley was right and she should wait even longer. . . .

Hearing her father's footsteps in the hall upstairs, Maddie quickly shoveled the last few bites of soggy cereal into her mouth. Then she typed another response.

[MADDIE] Not sure what I'll do yet—but I'll let u know this afternoon. Gtg—I don't want to be late!

[BROOKE] Have fun! And don't worry, everything will work out.

[NINA] Ya—the spirit of Misty is looking over u and Cloudy!

[HALEY] Wish we could all be there w/u!

[MADDIE] Me2! Will check in later. Bye!

She logged off and carried her bowl and spoon to the sink. By the time her father came into the kitchen, she was tying her boots.

"Ready to go?" her dad asked, grabbing the car keys off the counter.

Maddie felt a tiny shiver run down her spine. "I'm ready."

The barn was buzzing with activity when Maddie walked in. Just about every horse and pony was scheduled to go on the Snack & Swim ride—that meant nearly twenty riders would be getting ready at one time. Luckily, only about half of those riders had arrived so far, but the place was already a madhouse!

The twins were grooming their mounts in side-by-side crossties. Vic spotted Maddie and waved. "You're here! Hurry and put Cloudy in the crossties next to us."

"Okay." Maddie took two steps toward the mare's

stall, then stopped and turned around. "Actually, see if you can save the spot for me, okay? I—I need to talk to Ms. E about something first."

"Really?" Val said. She traded a look with her twin.

"You mean—*the* talk?" Vic added.

"Yeah." Maddie swallowed hard. "I'll be right back."

She hurried toward the office. Nina had been right—Maddie couldn't wait until after the ride. The suspense would only distract her from the day's fun. No, she had to talk to Ms. Emerson about buying Cloudy right away.

The barn owner was helping a teenage boarder untangle a bridle. She glanced up when Maddie approached.

"Oh, good, you're here," Ms. Emerson said. "Cloudy's waiting for you in her stall."

"Okay." Maddie took a deep breath. "Um, can I talk to you about something first? It's important." She glanced at the teen, who was fiddling with the bridle's throatlatch. "And sort of private."

Ms. Emerson looked surprised. She led the way to a quiet spot over by the wash stall. "Is something wrong, Madison?"

"No, not really." Maddie's mouth went dry and her

heart started pounding. "Uh, it's just that I've been think-ing about Cloudy, you know, and the Richardsons want-ing to buy her? And I—well, I think I want to buy her myself instead. If that's okay."

Ms. Emerson's eyebrows shot up. "Oh, Maddie . . . ," she began.

"No, listen, I'm serious about this," Maddie hurried on. "That's why I've been trying to earn money—I'll have enough for a down payment soon. And then I was think-ing maybe we could set up a payment plan? Like, I could pay you a certain amount every week or every month or whatever until she's all paid for. Oh! And I would want to board her here, of course—um, I guess I'd have to work out a payment plan for that, too. . . ."

"Maddie. Hold up for a second." Ms. Emerson put a hand on Maddie's arm. "Do your parents know about this plan of yours?"

Maddie gulped. "Um, not exactly. I mean, not yet. I mean, I was going to—that is, they think I—"

Ms. Emerson cut her off. "That's what I suspected. Look, Maddie, I appreciate how much you care about

Cloudy. But you have to realize it's not as simple as paying her off with your babysitting money."

Maddie frowned. "But I can get the money!" she protested. "Like I said, I've been looking for odd jobs, and I might start a dog-walking business, and . . ." Her voice trailed off as the barn owner held up a hand.

"Maddie, the thing is, you're a minor," Ms. Emerson said. "I would absolutely need to involve your parents before even considering selling her to you."

Maddie's heart dropped. "But—but you can't just let the Richardsons buy her instead," she argued. "You can't! Cloudy can't leave!"

The barn owner sighed, her expression softening. "Look, I really don't want to lose Cloudy, either." She shook her head. "That's why, when Mr. Richardson called me on Friday afternoon, I quoted him what I thought was a ridiculously high price."

"He called?" Maddie gulped. "So they definitely want to buy her?"

Ms. Emerson shrugged. "They seem quite determined. He was a bit taken aback by the price, I think, but he said he was sure we could work something out. Still, I—"

Just then a little girl rushed over, looking frantic. "Ms. E, Peaches won't let me catch her in the paddock, and I'm already late, and . . ."

"All right, all right. I'm coming." Ms. Emerson glanced at Maddie, looking concerned. "We can talk more later, Maddie. Just try not to worry about it, okay?"

Maddie nodded without speaking, biting the inside of her cheek to stop herself from crying. As soon as Ms. Emerson hurried off, Maddie raced in the other direction, not stopping until she reached Cloudy's stall.

The mare looked up from her hay and nickered. That was more than Maddie could take.

"Oh, Cloudy . . . ," she said, her voice wobbly and thick.

Burying her face in the pony's silky mane, she let the tears come. How could this be happening? It just wasn't fair. . . .

A few minutes later, she heard voices pass by right outside the stall, sounding happy and excited. That snapped her out of it. Sniffling back the last few tears, she wiped her face and forced a smile as Cloudy snuffled at her chest.

"Okay, got that out of my system," she told the pony as brightly as she could. "Now I might as well get over it and at least try to enjoy the ride."

Especially if it's the last chance I get to ride the best pony ever, she added silently.

To Maddie's surprise, she actually did manage to mostly forget the Richardson Situation and enjoy the ride. The Snack & Swim was just as much fun as she'd always imagined. The entire group, led by Ms. Emerson and Kiana and a couple of the adult boarders, headed out past the ring and down the hill to the trail winding between acres of irrigated farmland. They all laughed and talked and occasionally burst into song as they rode, and the horses and ponies seemed just as happy to be out as the humans.

Maddie and Cloudy were near the back of the group when they passed a house with a chain-link fence around the yard. Suddenly a flap in the front door opened and a wiry little dog raced out, barking at the top of its lungs.

The pony right in front of Cloudy spooked to one side,

their lawn, and Mr. Janicek had asked her to take Bosco to the park again. Other than that? Nothing. If things didn't pick up, it was going to take Maddie forever to earn enough money to buy Cloudy!

She picked at her food, barely hearing her sister's chatter about her super-important social plans for the weekend or Ry and Ty's arguments over who got the bigger pork chop.

"So, Mads," her father said, reaching for the salt. "Psyched for the big tryout tomorrow?"

"I guess." Maddie tried to sound more enthusiastic than she felt. "Don't get your hopes up, though, okay? Coach Wu says hardly anyone makes the cut their first time out."

Her father reached over and tugged on her hair. "Hardly anyone is as talented as my daughter."

Maddie's mother rolled her eyes. "Way to put pressure on the poor girl!"

But Maddie could tell her mother was joking. For some reason, she seemed just as excited as Maddie's dad about this whole Cascade League thing.

"Get real, Dad," Tyler said. "It'll be a miracle if Maddie makes it past the first cut."

Ryan looked up from his plate with a grin. "You know what's a miracle? That Mom and Dad actually convinced her to skip her prancy pony lesson to go to the tryout tomorrow."

Tyler snorted with laughter. "Yeah, that's a miracle all right—I thought they'd have to tie her up and throw her in the trunk of the car to get her away from the ponies! Prancy, prancy, prancy . . ."

"Whatever." Tillie speared a lima bean with her fork. "We all knew the horse thing wasn't going to last forever, right? I mean, this is Maddie we're talking about."

Maddie frowned as the rest of the family laughed. "Shut up," she told her sister. "I'm not the one who gave up all her other interests to start chasing boys like a pathetic loser."

"Maddie, that's enough!" her mother said sharply. "We're talking about you right now, not your sister. And you have to admit, you do have a history of being super-gung-ho about things and then giving them up cold turkey."

"Not this again," Maddie muttered. Would they ever get over the judo thing? "Riding's different."

"Okay." Tillie sounded skeptical. "Anyway, enough about that. Can someone drive me to the mall tomorrow morning?"

As the conversation wandered away from her, Maddie stared at her plate without really seeing it. Normally, her brothers' stupid jokes and insults didn't bother her. But for some reason she couldn't get Ryan's comment out of her head. Could he possibly be right? *Had* she given in too easily when her parents had insisted she skip her lesson to go to that tryout? She didn't usually defy her parents, but she could be stubborn when she felt strongly enough about something. When they'd packed up to move here from their previous home in Colorado, she'd locked herself in her room for almost an entire day until her parents had promised not to give away her beloved Flexible Flyer just because they were moving to a place where it never snowed.

But this time, she'd given up her lesson with barely a whimper. Did that mean she didn't feel as strongly about riding as she thought she did? Maybe it really was all about Cloudy. And now that she feared Cloudy might not be around much longer, maybe she was already starting to pull away. . . .

The thought made her feel anxious and uncertain, and she definitely didn't like feeling that way. Trying to shake it off, Maddie vowed to talk to Ms. Emerson as soon as possible. She'd just tell her the truth—she wanted to buy Cloudy, but she'd need some time to come up with the full amount. Maybe Nina could give her some tips on coming up with a payment plan. Or better yet, she could ask all her Pony Post friends for help—she knew Brooke had saved up to buy both her saddles, and Haley was always budgeting her allowance carefully to pay for her eventing lessons and competitions.

Having a plan made her feel better. With any luck, she'd be able to present her ideas to Ms. Emerson right after the Snack & Swim.

"By the way . . ." She spoke up suddenly, interrupting whatever Tillie was saying about her planned shopping spree. "Don't forget, I'll be gone all day Sunday at the Snack and Swim ride."

"The what?" Tillie wrinkled her nose.

nearly unseating its rider, the little girl with the black braids.

"Whoa! Are you okay, Prisha?" Val called out from behind Maddie.

The little girl let out a shriek as her pony backed away from the barking dog. "Stop, Tucker!" she cried, sounding scared. "Oh no!"

"It's okay, Prisha," Maddie called, urging Cloudy forward. The Chincoteague mare was staring at the dog too, but she seemed more curious than frightened. "Wait until I catch up, okay?"

She rode Cloudy up between the fence and the other pony. Prisha was clutching Tucker's mane, looking terrified.

"It's okay," Maddie said, reaching out to grab the little girl's rein. "We'll help you past it. Easy, Tucker—there's nothing to be worried about. . . ."

She kept talking soothingly to girl and pony as she legged Cloudy forward. Cloudy responded instantly, walking calmly past the noisy dog.

By this time, the riders ahead had stopped, realizing

something was happening. Ms. Emerson was standing in her stirrups, peering down the line.

"Is everything okay back there?" she called.

At that moment the house's front door opened and a college-age girl came out. "Spot!" she called. "Bad dog! Come!" As the dog stopped barking and bounded toward her, wagging its tail, the girl waved at the riders. "Sorry about that!"

Maddie smiled and dropped Cloudy's reins to wave back. "It's okay! Thanks!"

Soon the dog was inside and all the riders were safely past the house. As soon as the trail widened enough, Kiana caught up to Maddie.

"Well done, sweetie," she said, smiling down from her tall bay Thoroughbred's back. "You saved the day back there! It would've been a bummer to lose a rider this early, eh?"

Maddie grinned. "Not on my watch—or Cloudy's, either." As she bent to pat the steady little mare on the neck, the Richardsons crept back into her mind and her good mood wavered slightly. But she quickly banished them again, determined not to let them ruin the day.

After about an hour, Maddie and the rest of the riders reached a public park. It felt good to get out of the sun into the shade of the trees. They followed a winding dirt trail downhill, with the sound of rushing water growing louder with every step.

When they finally came within sight of the creek, Maddie gasped. "Wow, it's gorgeous!" she exclaimed.

"I know, right?" Vic grinned as she stopped her pony beside Cloudy. "Looks nice and cool, too."

Ms. Emerson let out a sharp whistle. "All right, everyone!" she called. "There are only two rules to remember before you go in the water. First, remove your saddles and set them over there." She waved toward some picnic tables on the bank. "Second, keep your helmets on at all times." She grinned. "The rest of your wardrobe is up to you. Now go have fun!"

Maddie cheered along with the others. She dismounted quickly, pulling off Cloudy's saddle. Then she stripped down to her swimsuit and climbed back on, bareback and barefoot, with the help of one of the picnic tables.

"Ready to cool off, Cloudy?" she said. "Let's go for a swim!"

She rode the pony into the creek. It was shallow along the edge, and Cloudy stopped as soon as her front feet were in the water, lowering her head for a nice long drink.

When she finished, Maddie kicked her on, aiming for the deeper water in the middle. Several horses and ponies were already out there, splashing around happily.

"Yipes!" Maddie yelped as Cloudy waded deep enough for her rider's legs to hit the water. "It's cold!"

Vic was right behind her on her pony. "I know. It feels great!" she said with a laugh.

"I hope that girl riding Peanut doesn't go too deep," Val said. "That pony is so short, he'll probably have to actually swim!"

"Do you have to worry about everything?" Vic asked her sister with a grin. "Because I'll give you something to worry about!" Leaning over, she tried to push Val off her pony into the water.

Val squawked and grabbed her pony's mane, clinging tightly with her legs. Her pony seemed to think she was supposed to go faster and leaped forward into the deepest part of the water.

Vic shouted with laughter as Val shrieked. "They say it doesn't feel as cold if you just jump right in!" Vic called.

Maddie was laughing too. "Oh yeah? Let's see how you like it!" She leaned over and gave Vic a shove. Vic was laughing so hard she didn't have a chance—she tipped right off her pony into the water.

"Oh, you'll pay for that, Martinez!" she sputtered as she came up for air. Swimming around her pony, she grabbed Maddie's ankle.

"Hey!" Maddie protested, trying to pull away.

But Vic gave a sharp yank. Maddie held on as tightly as she could, but Cloudy's back was slippery and she felt herself sliding . . . sliding . . .

SPLASH!

The water closed over her head, cool and refreshing. Maddie was grinning when she emerged. Cloudy's reins were still in her hand, and she followed them back to her pony's side.

"Good girl, Cloudy—stand still," she said, scrambling

back onto the pony's back. Vic was already back on her pony as well, though Val seemed content to paddle around in the water and blow bubbles in front of her pony.

Vic grinned at Maddie, pushing back a wet strand of hair that had escaped from under her helmet. "Race you to the other side?"

"You're on!" Maddie grinned, giving Cloudy a squeeze with her legs. "Come on, girl! You're a Chincoteague pony—you'd better not let them beat us at a swimming race!"

After an hour or so, Ms. Emerson called everyone out of the water. Once the horses and ponies were grazing in a fenced meadow near the creek, the riders all gathered around the picnic tables. An adult boarder's husband had brought over the picnic lunch in his car and set it up while everyone was swimming. There was a big platter of hot dogs, along with various cold salads, chips, rolls, cookies, and all kinds of other food.

"Wow, everything looks great!" Vic exclaimed as she piled a paper plate with potato salad and chocolate chip cookies.

"Yeah." Maddie grabbed a roll. "Swimming always makes me hungry."

Val popped a baby carrot into her mouth. "Let's not sit at the table," she said. "I saw a good spot over this way...."

She led them to a dappled clearing filled with wildflowers and a view of the area where their ponies were grazing. "Perfect!" Vic exclaimed.

Maddie just nodded, her eyes trained on Cloudy. The mare's sleek, damp palomino coat gleamed in the sun, and her mane and tail still dripped with moisture. For a second Maddie felt as if she'd been whisked off to the opposite coast and was looking at a wild pony that had just stepped out of the deep, chilly waters of the Assateague Channel.

Then she blinked, and it was just Cloudy again—*her* Cloudy, the best pony ever.

"Hey," Vic said, poking her in the arm. "So did you talk to Ms. Emerson about your plan?"

Maddie glanced around to make sure nobody else was close enough to hear. "Um, sort of. She said she can't sell her to me unless I talk to my parents first."

Val looked worried. "Okay. What do you think they'll say?"

"They'll probably be all over it." Vic licked some mustard off her finger. "I mean, they know how special Cloudy is. They won't want her to leave either, right?"

Maddie smiled weakly. "I guess. But listen, can we talk about this later? I—I kind of just want to focus on right now, if you know what I mean."

"Sure," Vic said, trading a slightly confused look with Val. "I guess."

When everyone had finished eating, the horses and ponies were almost dry. Maddie and the rest of the riders saddled up, mounted, and headed for home. By the time they climbed the hill behind the arena, Maddie's leg muscles were tired, her soggy ponytail was sticking to her back, and she was pretty sure her arms were sunburned.

But she was feeling good. The Snack & Swim had been just as much fun as she'd expected. Cloudy had been perfect, leading the other pony past that barking dog, wading right into the creek, and basically not putting a hoof wrong the entire ride. Then again, Maddie wouldn't have expected anything less.

"You really are a rock star, aren't you?" she murmured, giving Cloudy a pat as they crested the hill and came within sight of the arena.

Then Maddie froze as she saw a tall, lean figure standing right outside the barn. It was Mr. Richardson. And he was staring right at Cloudy.

⋄ CHAPTER ⋄
12

"WHAT'S *HE* DOING HERE?" VIC HISSED, riding up beside Maddie.

"I don't know, but he looks kind of impatient," Val said.

Maddie couldn't say a word. She was tempted to turn Cloudy around and gallop back down the trail, hiding her away somewhere until the Richardsons gave up their crazy idea about buying her.

But she knew that wouldn't work. If Mr. Richardson was here to finalize the sale, there was nothing she could do about it. It was too late. All her plans had failed, and she was going to lose Cloudy. She dug her fingers into the mare's mane, tangling the silky pale hair around her hand, feeling as if her heart might break.

"Come on, Cloudy," she choked out, sliding down from the saddle. "I'd better get you untacked and cleaned up."

"Maddie . . . ," Val began.

Maddie didn't respond except to shake her head. She couldn't say another word, or she might totally lose it.

The twins seemed to understand, letting her hurry off without them. Maddie was glad. She didn't want to be with anyone right now—except Cloudy.

Back in Cloudy's stall, Maddie stripped off the saddle and bridle and dumped them in the aisle right outside. Ms. Emerson would be annoyed if she noticed the tack sitting on the floor, but Maddie didn't care. She wanted to spend every second she could with Cloudy—grooming her, giving her treats, scratching all her itchy spots, and thanking her for being so amazing for the past year and a half.

About fifteen minutes later, Maddie heard footsteps stop outside the stall. She glanced up as Ms. Emerson poked her head in over the half door.

"What is it?" Maddie snapped. She knew she sounded

rude, but she couldn't help it. It was too soon! Couldn't she have more time? Even ten minutes—five?

Ms. Emerson had a strange expression on her face. "Maddie," she said. "I just had a very interesting talk with Mr. Richardson." She took a deep breath. "As it happens, the family isn't interested in buying Cloudy after all."

Maddie blinked, not sure she'd heard her right. "What?" she cried so loudly that Cloudy flinched and took a step away from her.

"That's right. It seems the Richardsons got a last-minute invitation from some family friends to go skiing in the mountains yesterday. That's why they didn't show up for their riding lesson." The barn owner shrugged. "And after a day on the slopes, apparently the whole family is hooked. They've decided to focus their time and funds on getting involved in that sport right now."

"Whoa!" Maddie just stood there, trying to take in what the barn owner was telling her. Part of her wanted to jump around and scream with joy. Cloudy was staying!

But another part didn't dare to celebrate quite yet.

Amber might be willing to give up riding for skiing, and the rest of the family too. But Filly Richardson was definitely, genuinely, hopelessly horse crazy—Maddie could tell, since she was exactly the same way herself. No, Filly wasn't likely to give up her pony dreams permanently. And the Richardsons were pretty flaky—what if they got tired of skiing after a few weeks or months and came around, wanting to buy Cloudy again?

Ms. Emerson was watching Maddie closely. "You don't have to worry, Maddie," she said. "The truth is, I wasn't going to sell Cloudy back to the Richardsons regardless."

"What?" Maddie blinked, not getting it. What had all the fuss been about over the past week? "But I thought—"

"I didn't really want to sell Cloudy at all—she's a valuable part of the barn and would be difficult to replace." Ms. Emerson folded her arms and leaned on the stall's half door. "Plus, given the Richardsons' past with the mare, I had my doubts all along, to say the least. But they begged me to consider their offer, so I figured I'd give them a chance to prove they'd learned their lesson and intended to become more responsible horse owners this time around." She grimaced. "It didn't take me long to realize that wasn't the case."

"Yeah." Maddie thought back to the careless way Amber had acted around Cloudy—as if she already knew everything there was to know about ponies and riding.

The barn owner nodded. "I probably should have told them it wasn't going to work out as soon as I figured it out. I guess I was just hoping that spending some time here, taking a few lessons, might make them think twice about rushing out to buy another green horse or pony—or, who knows, maybe even flying back out to Chincoteague next month for the pony auction."

For a moment, Maddie was too stunned to speak. Then a big grin spread across her face. "I never would've guessed you were such a sneak!" she exclaimed. Then, seeing Ms. Emerson raise an eyebrow, she quickly added, "Um, I mean that as a compliment, okay?"

"Hmm." Ms. Emerson pursed her lips. "Well, are you just going to stand there, grinning like a loon? Or are you going to actually groom that poor filthy pony?" She waved a hand at Cloudy. "There's more to being a horsewoman than just riding, you know."

Maddie's grin widened, threatening to split her face in two. "Yes, ma'am." She saluted crisply, just as she'd seen her mother do a zillion times. "I'm on it, ma'am."

"That's more like it." Ms. Emerson's expression remained stern, but her eyes twinkled. "I'll leave you to it, then."

As the barn owner hurried off, Maddie flung her arms around Cloudy's neck. "Did you hear that, girl?" she exclaimed. "You're staying!"

She was so happy and relieved she could barely stand it. Her mind raced, imagining all the fun she was going to have this summer—and beyond—with the best pony ever to swim the Assateague Channel.

Maddie's laptop chimed. She pulled it closer on the bed, peering at the screen. A new post had just appeared.

[HALEY] I'm here! Nina just called and ordered me to get online. What's going on?

[NINA] Took u long enough!!! Maddie won't tell us what happened on her ride today until we're all here.

[BROOKE] Ya—and we've been dying of curiosity! So spill it already, M! Was the S&S amazing?

Maddie smiled and opened a new text box. Nina and Brooke had been trying to convince her to tell them about her day ever since she'd logged on fifteen minutes earlier. But she wanted them all together when she gave them the news.

[MADDIE] The ride was great. I'll tell u all about it in a sec. But first, big news—Cloudy's staying!

[NINA] Wait, WUT?!?!?!?!?!?

[HALEY] OMG, r u serious?

[BROOKE] What happened?????

Maddie typed fast, giving them the basic story. The next few entries from her friends were a jumble of exclamations of joy, with plenty of careless typos and even more exclamation points.

Finally the excitement died down a little. Then a new post popped up.

[BROOKE] Wait, I almost forgot—what happened w/ the soccer thing? If u make the travel team, won't u have to stop riding for a while?

[MADDIE] O right, I almost forgot to tell u guys that part. I talked to my parents about it as soon as I got home from the barn.

[HALEY] What did u tell them?

[MADDIE] I said I didn't want to give up riding to do the C. League. I love soccer, and I still want to play on my reg. team. But I love riding even more. I don't want to give it up, even for 1 summer.

[NINA] Good for u! What did they say?

Maddie smiled, still surprised by her parents' reaction. That was at least partly thanks to her Pony Post friends— she'd applied some of the tips they'd given her for talking to Ms. Emerson to the conversation with her parents. And it had worked. Her parents had been impressed with the grown-up way Maddie presented her arguments. They were disappointed, of course—they still thought playing for the Cascade League would be a good opportunity. But they'd agreed that it should be Maddie's choice and had agreed to call the league to withdraw her name from consideration.

[MADDIE] They said it was OK. They want me to be happy.

[NINA] And we all know Cloudy makes u happy!

[BROOKE] Ya. Chinc. ponies are amazing!

[**HALEY**] Definitely!

Maddie smiled, thinking again about all the fun times she had to look forward to with Cloudy.

[**MADDIE**] Long live Chincoteague ponies!

• Glossary •

Chincoteague pony: A breed of pony found on Assateague Island, which lies off the coasts of Maryland and Virginia. Chincoteague ponies are sometimes referred to as wild horses, but are more properly called "feral" since they are not native to the island but were brought there by humans sometime many years past. There are several theories about how this might have happened, including the one told in the classic novel *Misty of Chincoteague* by Marguerite Henry. That novel also details the world-famous pony swim and auction that still take place in the town of Chincoteague to this day.

aids: The cues given by a rider to a horse or pony, such as squeezing with the legs to ask for more speed or pulling on the reins to request the animal to slow or halt. Both horses and riders must be taught what these aids mean.

breeches: Pants specially designed for horseback riding. They come in a variety of styles but often have patches of leather or other material to protect the rider's legs.

buckskin: A color of horse or pony. Buckskins have a coat that is light brown, yellowish, tan, or gold, with black legs, mane, and tail.

chestnut: This term has two horse-related meanings: (1) a horse color; chestnuts can be various shades of red, with manes and tails of the same or lighter hue and no black points; (2) the callous-like spots on the inside of a horse's front legs, believed to be a vestigial toe.

crossrail: A type of jump with two poles that cross in the middle to form an X shape. Crossrails are usually very low, with a clear midpoint, and thus often used for beginners (riders and horses alike) who are first learning to jump.

dressage: A sport in which horse and rider perform a series of movements in the ring, known as "tests." Dressage is one of the three equestrian disciplines seen in the summer Olympic Games along with show jumping and eventing.

farrier: Also known as a horseshoer or blacksmith, a farrier takes care of horses' feet by trimming them on a regular basis (they are always growing, just like human fingernails) and applying shoes if needed.

foal: A baby horse or pony.

gelding: A neutered male horse or pony.

girth: The strap that goes around a horse or pony's barrel—rib cage area—to hold a saddle in place. (Western riders call this piece of tack a "cinch.")

lunge line (or longe line): A long rope used to exercise and train horses and ponies from the ground. The person holding the lunge line stands still while the animal moves around him or her in a circle. A horse or pony can also be lunged/longed with a rider on it.

mare: An adult female horse or pony. (A young female is called a "filly.")

palomino: A color of horse or pony. Palominos have a cream, gold, or yellowish coat with a white mane and tail.

pinto: A type of horse coloring consisting of spots of white and a second color. Pintos are common in the Chincoteague pony breed—Misty was a palomino pinto.

tack: The equipment used in riding or driving a horse or pony, such as a saddle, bridle, harness, or reins. Putting this equipment on a horse or pony is known as "tacking up," and taking it off is "untacking."

Thoroughbred: A breed of horse used in horse racing, as well as in almost every other riding sport and discipline.

weanling: A young horse or pony that has recently been separated from its mother. The horse or pony will typically be referred to as a weanling until it turns a year old, at which time it will be called a yearling.

Marguerite Henry's Ponies of Chincoteague is inspired by the award-winning books by Marguerite Henry, the beloved author of such classic horse stories as *King of the Wind*; *Misty of Chincoteague*; *Justin Morgan Had a Horse*; *Stormy, Misty's Foal*; *Misty's Twilight*; and *Album of Horses*, among many other titles.

Learn more about the world of Marguerite Henry at www.MistyofChincoteague.org.

Don't miss the next book in the series!

Book 2: *Blue Ribbon Summer*

BROOKE RHODES YAWNED AND POKED HER glasses farther up her nose as she walked across her backyard. It was early, probably not even seven thirty, though Brooke wasn't sure, since she'd forgotten to put on her watch. Already, though, the heat made her feel lazy and sluggish, as if she should kick off her sneakers and cool her feet in the dew-damp grass.

There was a muffled thump from inside the small barn at the back of the tidy patch of lawn. Swallowing another yawn, Brooke hurried forward and shoved at the barn door. It resisted, remaining stubbornly shut. The humidity, Brooke's stepfather said. He'd promised all last summer to sand down the door so it worked better, but the chore had never quite made it to the top of his to-do list. Brooke wasn't holding her breath for this summer either.

Another thump came from inside the barn, followed by a surprisingly deep nicker. Brooke smiled.

"Relax, Foxy girl. I'm coming," she called.

She shoved harder and the door finally gave way, letting Brooke into the tiny barn. Well, Brooke liked to call it a barn, anyway. The Amish builders who'd come from St. Mary's County to put it up had referred to it as a shed. It was a long, low wooden structure with a corrugated metal roof. Half of it was enclosed into a combination feed, tack, and general storage room, while the other half was an open stall where Foxy could come in out of the rain, heat, or wind, and where her food and water buckets hung. Brooke liked to call the two sections the pony part and the people part.

Foxy was staring over the Dutch door between the two halves, ears pricked, when Brooke let herself into the people part of the barn. "Don't worry, breakfast is coming," Brooke said, reaching out to rub the pony's nose as she hurried past. "Just hang on. . . ."

She grabbed her battered old feed scoop and opened the metal trash can in the corner that held Foxy's grain. The scoop had been a gift from the neighbors when Foxy had first come home four years earlier, and Brooke wouldn't have replaced it with a newer or fancier one even if she could afford to, because it reminded her of that day—one of the best of her life. She scooped out the proper amount of feed in one expert movement and headed for the Dutch door.

"Out of the way, Foxy." Brooke poked the pony in the chest, and Foxy moved aside as Brooke let herself into the stall area. After dumping the feed into Foxy's pink plastic bucket, Brooke stepped back to allow the mare to dive in.

Brooke stood with Foxy for a moment, a hand on the pony's glossy chestnut shoulder. This was always one of her favorite times of the day. It was even better now that school was out and Brooke didn't have to rush off to meet the bus.

"What should we do today, girl?" Brooke murmured, picking absently at a spot of dried mud on the pony's coat. "Maybe go for a ride before it gets too hot?"

Foxy flicked an ear her way, though she didn't lift her

head from the bucket. Brooke's gaze wandered out the open front of the shed. The sun was already burning the last of the dew off the grass. On the far side of Foxy's three-acre pasture, Brooke saw that the neighbors' retired draft horses had already taken up residence under the big oak tree on the property line, dozing and flicking their tails against the flies. It was going to be a hot one. Maybe it would be better to wait and ride after dinner.

A few minutes later Brooke let herself into the house through the back door. The kitchen smelled like coffee and toast. On the TV tucked under the cherrywood cabinets, a local newscaster was blabbering about the traffic. At the table, Brooke's five-year-old twin brother and sister were chattering at each other, though Brooke couldn't hear what they were saying over the sound of her stepfather's booming voice. He was standing at the counter, his cell phone pressed to his ear with one hand while he fiddled with the coffee maker with the other.

Stepping over to the toaster, Brooke grabbed the bread someone had left nearby. Her mother glanced at her.

"Oh, sweetie," she said. "There you are. What's on

your agenda for today? Are you okay staying by yourself for a while? I've got an open house in . . ." She glanced at her gold watch and her eyes widened. "Less than forty minutes. I've got to go!"

At that moment Brooke's stepfather hung up the phone. "I'm off," he told his wife, stepping over to give her a peck on the cheek. "Got a hot lead on someone looking for a classic Corvette, and they want to come in right now."

"Can you drop the twins off at day camp on your way to the lot?" Brooke's mother asked. "I'm running late."

"Sure." Brooke's stepfather ruffled Ethan's hair. "Come on, twins. First one to the garage gets to ride shotgun."

Brooke's mother rolled her eyes. "No shotgun! I keep telling you, Roger, they're too young. Backseat only, you two. In your car seats, straps buckled." She bustled over to the table, efficiently packing Ethan and Emma into their Velcro sandals and sun hats.

Brooke's stepfather grabbed his keys. "Need me to drop you off anywhere, Brooke?" he asked.

"No thanks." Brooke shrugged. "I was just going to hang around here today. Maybe go for a ride or something."

"Good, good." Brooke could tell her stepfather wasn't really listening. He had his cell phone out again, scrolling through the messages.

Moments later the others were gone and Brooke had the house to herself. She wandered over to switch off the TV, waving a hand to shoo away the flies buzzing over the crumbs the twins had left everywhere. Why did it sometimes feel as if her family forgot she was even around?

She shrugged off the thought. Her family was busy, that was all. Her stepfather's used car lot was the most successful one on the Eastern Shore of Maryland. *Let Rhodes put you on the road*—that was his slogan, and everyone Brooke met seemed to know it. Sometimes she wished she still had her old last name, Bradley. But when Brooke was six years old, her stepfather had officially adopted her, and her mother had insisted they all have the same last name, saying that would help make them a family. Brooke didn't really mind, especially since her real father had died when she was too young to remember him. But she sometimes wished she'd at least been given a choice.

That was how Brooke's mother did things, though.

When she made a decision, she stuck to it: no second thoughts. She was the type of person who couldn't stay still for more than two minutes at a time unless she was asleep. She'd gone back to selling real estate the moment the twins started preschool, and when she wasn't at the office or visiting a sale property, she was tidying her own house or shopping or doing any of the zillion other things she did every day.

Brooke got tired just thinking about it. She definitely hadn't inherited her mom's energy level or need to be involved in everything. In fact, she loved nothing more than spending an entire afternoon lying in the grass watching Foxy graze, or curling up for hours to read a book, whether it was a horse care or training manual or her very favorite classic story, *Misty of Chincoteague*. Brooke had read the story of the Beebe children and their special pony so many times that every page was dog-eared and the cover was starting to come loose.

The ding of the toaster broke Brooke out of her thoughts. Grabbing her toast, she tossed it onto a plate, then poured herself a glass of orange juice. Wandering into the den, she set her breakfast down next to the computer. The screen was a lot bigger than the one on her laptop, and she was hoping Maddie had put more photos on the Pony Post.

The Pony Post was a private online message board with just four members. Brooke had never met the other three in person, but she considered them among her best friends. Over the past year and a half, the four of them had bonded over their shared love of Chincoteague ponies.

Maddie Martinez had been the one to come up with the idea of the site. She lived in northern California and rode a Chincoteague mare named Cloudy who was the spitting image of the original Misty. Maddie was the type of person Brooke wished she could be—active, outgoing, and fun-loving.

Then there was Nina Peralt. She lived in New Orleans with her parents and owned a pony named Bay Breeze. She was one of the coolest people Brooke knew—sociable and artsy and smart—and her whole big-city existence seemed very sophisticated compared to Brooke's life.

The final member was Haley Duncan, who lived on a small farm in Wisconsin. Her pony was a spunky gelding named Wings that Haley leased from a neighbor. Haley was bold and determined and focused, which were all traits that Brooke guessed were very necessary for Haley's chosen sport of eventing.

Sometimes Brooke's friend Adam made fun of her "imaginary friends," as he called them. But Brooke couldn't imagine life without Maddie, Nina, Haley, and the Pony Post.

Brooke chewed a bite of toast as she logged on to the Internet. Soon the familiar Pony Post logo popped up. It showed four Chincoteague ponies galloping through the surf on Assateague Island, which was only an hour or so down the coast from where Brooke was sitting at that very moment.

Quite a few new posts had appeared since Brooke had checked in the evening before. There were several new photos, too, just as she'd hoped. Maddie had participated in a special trail ride at her barn the previous weekend, and she'd been sharing photos ever since.

[MADDIE] Check it out, guys—my friends e-mailed me more pix from the Snack & Swim. Vic even got one of me diving off Cloudy's back! Hope you like them!

[NINA] Fab photos! Wish we could do something like that at my barn. But I guess we'd have to swim in the Mississippi River, lol! Probably not such a brilliant idea.

[HALEY] LOL! Def. not. We don't want u and Breezy to get swept out into the Gulf of Mexico!

[NINA] No worries, we already know all our ponies can swim, right?

Brooke smiled as she read her friends' comments. Their ponies' special heritage was what had originally drawn the Pony Post members together. But only Brooke had actually seen her pony swim across the channel between Assateague and Chincoteague islands during the annual pony penning. That was almost four years ago, when Brooke was barely eight years old, but she remembered it as if it had happened yesterday.

Brooke had loved horses and ponies for as long as she could remember. She'd started riding at age five on the neighbors' gentle, patient draft horses, and had taken weekly riding lessons the summer she was seven, though somehow there hadn't seemed to be enough time or money to continue after the twins came along. Brooke had dreamed of her own pony for so long that when her parents had finally agreed to let her use her saved-up allowance and birthday money to buy one at the Chincoteague pony auction, Brooke had barely dared to believe it.

Actually, Foxy hadn't been her first choice. Brooke had hoped to find a pinto like the famous Misty. She'd stayed at the pony pens long after her parents had lost interest and wandered off to find something to eat, looking over each spindly-legged foal and taking notes to help herself remember which were her favorites. She'd spotted a sweet-faced bay filly with markings similar to Misty's, and a little buckskin colt with bold white splashes on both sides. Those had been her favorites, though Brooke had also picked out two or three other cute spotted foals.

Then the pony auction had started. When the bay filly's turn came, Brooke never even got the chance to bid. The opening bid was double the total amount she had to spend. Within seconds, other bidders had jumped in, and Brooke didn't even hear the final price.

"Never mind, sweetie," her mother had said. "You can try for the next one."

But the buckskin colt had sold for triple Brooke's top price, and the others for more than that. Even the solid-colored foals were more expensive than she could afford.

Finally there were only a few young ponies left. One of them was a gangly yearling filly that Brooke had barely noticed in the pens, a chestnut with a lighter mane and tail. She didn't fit Brooke's idea of the perfect Chincoteague pony. But she had a soft eye and a calm temperament, and at that moment, that had been enough for Brooke to raise her hand when the auctioneer called for bids. Brooke had never regretted ending up with Foxy—or forgotten the way her stepfather had kicked in an extra hundred dollars at the last minute so Brooke could buy her.

Brooke smiled as she thought back to that exciting day, even as she continued to scan the rest of the new entries on the Pony Post.

[NINA] What are you and Cloudy up to now that the Snack & Swim is over? And how about the rest of you? Haley, Brooke?

[MADDIE] Back to reg. lessons. Ms. Emerson says we're going to start doing some jumping gymnastics. Should be fun! I love jumping, and so does Cloudy!!

[NINA] Cool! I just started doing more jumping too, mostly b/c I found out my barn is having a show this fall. There's going to be a costume class too! Can't wait to think of ideas for that!!

[HALEY] Excellent! What other classes will u enter?

[NINA] Not sure yet—my instructor says we'll

figure it out by the end of the summer. What about

u, Haley? Got any events coming up or anything?

[HALEY] Wings and I have big plans for this

summer. I have almost enough $ saved

up for another lesson w/ my XC coach.

[MADDIE] XC? That's cross-country,

right? Like jumping over big giant logs

and other scary stuff like that?

[HALEY] LOL! It's not that scary—it's

fun! U should try it sometime . . .

Brooke scanned the rest of the entries. Nina and
Maddie asked Haley more questions about eventing, then
added more about their own lessons. They all had such big
plans for themselves and their ponies for the summer!

And what plans do I have? Brooke wondered, nibbling
at her toast, which had gone cold as she read. Nothing.

Just riding around the neighborhood trying not to get sunburned or eaten alive by mosquitoes and blackflies. Big whoop.

She sighed. It wasn't as if she had much choice. Lessons and shows cost money, and Brooke never seemed to have enough of that. She'd recently spent everything she'd saved up from her allowance and the past couple months of odd jobs—washing cars at the lot, feeding the neighbors' drafts when they went out of town, the occasional babysitting gig—on fly spray and horse treats, a new hoofpick to replace the one she'd lost somehow and a new halter to replace the one Foxy had broken. There never seemed to be an end to the expenses a pony could run up!

Still, Brooke knew she should stop feeling sorry for herself. She was lucky to have a pony at all. She was lucky her parents had helped her buy Foxy, and that they paid for the pony's basic needs, even if her stepfather still grumbled every time he swiped his credit card at the feed store or wrote a check to the farrier who trimmed Foxy's hooves.

She skimmed her friends' posts again. Their summer

plans sounded so exciting. But why should they have all the fun? Even if Brooke and Foxy wouldn't be showing— or even taking lessons—anytime soon, that didn't mean they couldn't train as if they were. Right?

Brooke's mood brightened as she turned the idea over in her head. She owned a whole shelf full of books about horses and riding, and there were more in the library, not to mention plenty of videos online. She'd done most of Foxy's training herself so far, with lots of research and advice from her neighbors and others. And Foxy was five now—old enough to do anything Brooke wanted to do with her. So why not get more serious about their training? It would be fun!

"Thanks, guys," Brooke murmured, closing the Pony Post page. She'd wait and update her friends later. Right now she was eager to head back out to the barn and get started on her own big plans.

Brooke dropped her dishes in the sink, then went back outside. It was hotter already, and the drone of insects filled the air. Brooke grabbed Foxy's halter as she entered through the people part of the barn, then headed out into the pasture. Foxy was grazing in her favorite spot right across the fence from the draft horses' shade tree. She lifted her head when Brooke called her, then ambled over to meet her owner.

"Hey, girl," Brooke whispered, running her hand up the pony's sleek reddish-brown neck to scratch her favorite spot. "Ready to become a show horse?"

Foxy curled her neck, her lower lip flopping with pleasure as she leaned into the scratch. After a moment Brooke slid the halter onto Foxy's head, then led her over to the hitching ring in the run-in stall.

"Be right back," Brooke said, giving the mare a pat. She hurried back into the people part of the barn. She kept her grooming tools in a bucket that had held Foxy's water for the first few months Brooke had owned her. That winter, the bucket had cracked in the first hard freeze, and Brooke had had to beg her parents for the money to replace it with a rubber one. But the plastic one still worked fine to hold her grooming stuff.

Soon she was hard at work brushing the dirt out of Foxy's coat and picking burrs and twigs out of her mane and tail. By the time the mare was halfway clean, Brooke was sweaty and panting as if she'd just run halfway to Salisbury. The thought of lugging her saddle out of the barn and tacking up made her want to lie down and take a nap in the shade.

"Maybe it's too hot to start our training right now," she told Foxy, who had one hind foot cocked and appeared to be half asleep. Brooke glanced down at herself, realizing something else. "Besides, I forgot to change clothes."

She'd ridden countless times in her current outfit of shorts and tennis shoes, but rarely in a saddle. The leathers of her English saddle always pinched her bare legs, and the fenders on her battered old Western one rubbed.

Brooke hesitated, glancing toward the house. It wouldn't take long to run inside and change into jeans and paddock boots. But was it really worth it on such a hot day?

Instead, she ducked into the people part just long enough to grab her plastic schooling helmet and Foxy's bridle. Moments later, she was slipping on to Foxy bare-back from the fence rail. She glanced at the humble riding ring she'd laid out in one corner of the pasture, then tugged on one rein to turn Foxy in the other direction.

"It's no big deal," she murmured, rubbing the mare's withers as they set out along the edge of the soybean field next door. "We can start our training tomorrow."